MW00465861

HONORING LENA

A SWEET ROMANTIC SUSPENSE

SARA BLACKARD

Copyright © 2021 Sara Blackard

For more information on this book and the author visit: https://www.sarablackard.com

Editor Raneé S. Clark with Sweetly Us Press.

All rights reserved.

No part of this book may be reproduced in any form or by any electronic or mechanical means, including information storage and retrieval systems, without written permission from the author, except for the use of brief quotations in a book review.

This is a work of fiction. Names, characters, and incidents are all products of the author's imagination or are used for fictional purposes.

ONE

THE MELODIC SOUND of laughter shot Marshall Rand's gaze across the Siné Irish Pub in Arlington, Virginia. It had been a mistake choosing this place with all its memories. The instant he'd walked through the door and seen the happy couple at his and Amara's spot, he'd regretted giving in to nostalgia and having his assistant, Ed, set up the meeting there with the new investor instead of in DC. He didn't need the memories his murdered wife's favorite restaurant resurrected to keep him moving forward with his goals. He had all the incentive he needed just looking in his son's big brown eyes that looked just like his mom's.

"So, do we have a deal?" Patrick Walker, the CEO for Moving Forward, asked as he rubbed his mouth with his napkin.

Marshall pulled his gaze from the couple and extended his hand across the table. "I look forward to working with you."

Despite Marshall's distraction, the meeting had been a success. With Moving Forward coming on as an investor to his manufacturing company, he'd be able to build another warehouse in Texas completely dedicated to the products they created for June Rivas's inventions. The savings in freight and ability to have their researchers work more closely would benefit even more troops the inventions went to.

The more units equipped with the Eyes Beyond and latest body armor suit June had created, the more lives saved. The more lives saved, the more guilt Marshall could lift from his shoulders. At least, he hoped that would be the case.

Patrick glanced at his watch, his eyes widening. "Well then, I've got another meeting to get to. I'll have paper-work sent over for you to look at." He clapped Ed, who sat next to him, on the shoulder. "Thanks for a great lunch, boys."

"Any time." Marshall nodded as Patrick stood and headed for the door.

With that meeting out of the way, Marshall turned to his assistant, Ed. "Where are we with Senator Hammond?"

"Can't you bask in success for a minute?" Ed Ross, Marshall's assistant and best friend since college, shook his head and motioned toward Patrick's receding form. "He hasn't even made it out the door, and you're already on to the next conquest."

"The vote on the term limit bill is less than a week away." Marshall poked at the last of his lunch. "We need Hammond behind it if it has a chance of passing."

Ed pointed his chicken wing at Marshall, dripping Siné's signature sauce on the table. "You'll never get him to back the bill if you don't offer him something in return."

"I don't mind supporting him and his plans," Marshall said, his voice firm. "But that benefit he's hosting puts money directly into pockets I refuse to fill."

Ed grimaced at Marshall like he was a petulant child. "You and your high horse."

"I won't compromise my beliefs, Ed." Marshall stabbed a bite of his banger with his fork and scooped it through the last of his garlic potatoes. "Not again."

His gaze darted back to the table that held so many memories before he forced himself to focus on his meal. He needed to remember in the future when nostalgia hit to smother it. Nothing but regret and heartache filled the past, and tormenting himself with Amara's favorite hangouts while they visited this cesspool called the Capitol only made things worse.

His stomach hardened with grief, and he set his fork on the plate. He stared out the window as Ed sulked over his wings. A mother pulled her son down the sidewalk. The boy had blonde hair sticking in all directions like Marshall's son did. The two boys looked about the same age. The reminder of Carter softened the rock of grief lodged in Marshall's stomach.

The past hadn't just left sorrow and agony behind. Carter lived as a testament to Marshall's love for Amara. Marshall would do everything in his power to be the man of character Carter deserved—to be a better father than he had been a husband.

"Marsh, listen." Ed pushed his plate to the edge of the table and rested his forearms on the empty space.

His face took on that look he got when someone tested his tenacity. The expression had always marveled Marshall, causing him to settle in for whatever heated debate Ed would get into. Marshall resented being on the receiving end of Ed's bull-doggedness. If the man wasn't Marshall's closest friend, the pushing would end up with a termination notice.

"If you don't bend some, this trip will be a complete waste." Ed squeezed his hands together. "You can't make change without compromise."

Marshall had stubbornness to match. He hadn't won the Kentucky congressional seat on his good looks alone—hadn't taken Amara's already prosperous company and shot it into the stratosphere of success. He hired Ed to be the balance he needed in these situations, but it rankled that he'd have to explain to him again.

"I compromise plenty." Marshall tossed his napkin on his half-eaten meal and leaned back in his chair, his gaze darting to his head of security, Tony, sitting a table over as he put his hand to his ear and nodded. "I can't put my support behind Hammond's fundraiser, not with my questions unanswered."

"It's the Cry Out Against Human Trafficking organization, for Pete's sake. How could you possibly be against helping those victims?"

"I'm not against helping, and you know that." Marshall's chest heated at the accusation. "I'm just not convinced the organization is on the up and up. There are red flags waving that I can't ignore."

"I've read up on them, and they seem fine. Better than fine." Ed tapped his index finger on the table. "You won't get Hammond to budge. In fact, he may undo everything we've accomplished so far."

Marshall stared Ed down, though he inwardly cringed. Ed brought up some valid points. Was Marshall cutting himself off at the knees with his stubbornness? He shook his head with a sigh. Something didn't sit right with the organization. He had that twisting feeling in his gut that told him something was off. He'd ignored that instinct before, pushed it aside for the better good.

He stared back across the restaurant at the happy couple. Being a widower wasn't better *or* good. He promised himself he wouldn't ignore that warning bell again, no matter who it upset or if it made his end goal more difficult to obtain. He could dig his heels in with the best of them.

"It doesn't matter what Leland Hammond does or doesn't do." Marshall smiled at the server as she brought the check and he handed her his credit card before turning back to Ed with a weariness that ached his muscles. "I left Congress after Amara's murder because I refused to play the political game. Bending now isn't an option and never will be."

"Marsh, you have to let that go." Ed's eyes held concern. "Amara's accident, while tragic, can't hold you down and bind your options anymore."

"Murder." Heat rose up Marshall's neck, and he swallowed it down. "There was no accident."

"I know. I'm sorry." Ed shook his head and rubbed the back of his neck. "It's been two years. I don't want to see her death strangle you anymore. Eventually, it could choke out everything and leave you with nothing. Amara wouldn't want that."

A headache throbbed behind Marshall's eyes. Her death wasn't strangling him. It fueled him. Keeping it in the forefront of his mind propelled him to work harder. He'd make her family company he'd inherited into a name that others equated with influence and power, bolstering the nation's freedom he loved so much. Could wanting that as a monument to his wife be such a bad thing?

Could his drive to make up for his colossal mistakes kill everything good left in his life? Carter filled Marshall's mind. When was the last time he'd really played with his son? Sure, they saw each other every day, even bringing

Carter along when Marshall had to travel. But were the snatches of thirty minutes here and there enough? The three-year-old learned something new all the time, and Marshall barely had a moment to celebrate his son's milestones.

A pub employee set down the small folder with the credit card and receipt as they rushed past, and Marshall pushed the troubling thoughts aside. He could worry about his son and their relationship later. His focus had to remain on the task at hand—getting senators and congressmen to see reason and vote for limited terms. There had to be enough loyal to the republic to see that lifetime seats equated bad policy. When they all got back to Kentucky, he'd work in his schedule more time with Carter.

"I just ..." Ed sighed and met Marshall's gaze. "I just want what's best for you, man. I don't want you to crash in a blaze of glory when you could cruise into your goals."

Marshall really looked at his best friend across the table. Though he had just turned thirty-one like Marshall, Ed's hair was graying at his temples, and he appeared more worn around the edges than he should. Was that Marshall's fault as well? Had his desire to right his own past put unnecessary strain on his friend?

"Man, you know I'm not the cruisin' type." Marshall forced a laugh as he reached for his credit card. "But if it'll make you happy, I'll look into that organization again. Maybe I'm wrong."

Marshall opened the receipt holder and plucked up his card, his eyes skimming the handwritten note beneath the card. His hand froze, and the room closed in around him, blurring and slowing as he read the words again.

Do what we say or your son will end up like your wife.

"I know you'll never slow down, but at least y—" The

muffle of Ed's voice thawed Marshall's frozen muscles. "What? Marsh, what's wrong?"

Marshall picked up the note. His hand shaking made the paper flutter loudly in the air. Ed scanned the note and gulped. He lifted wide eyes to Marshall as his face paled.

"We're leaving." Marshall shoved his chair out so fast it crashed to the floor. "We're leaving now."

As he rushed to the door with the note bunched in his hand, he pulled out his phone and dialed Lena Rebel, Carter's bodyguard that posed as his nanny, scanning the restaurant for the employee that had dropped off the receipt. She wasn't anywhere in sight. In fact, he couldn't remember seeing her before that either. The sinking feeling from earlier hit him again as he glanced back to their table where Ed threw the pen after scribbling a signature on the charge slip.

The call connected, and Marshall didn't wait for Lena to talk. "Is Carter safe?"

"Yes. He's right here with me in the house." Lena's answer fired at him with the efficiency he'd come to expect from her.

Relief flooded through him. "Good. Keep him close. I'll be there shortly to explain."

Marshall hung up before she could answer and stomped out the pub door, his frigid shock turning to white-hot anger. He didn't understand what they wanted him to do, but no one threatened his family. Not again. He'd keep his family safe this time at all costs.

TWO

"EENA, ME NEEDS YOURS HELP." Carter Rand peered his big brown eyes up at Lena Rebel as he lifted the marker to her. "Pease."

He smiled, a look of such hopefulness on his face that Lena knew she'd break. Where had the tough, no-nonsense woman gone—the one who didn't put up with strife from anyone? Where was the soldier who'd pushed herself to be the best, leaving men in the dust as she did? Where had the army medic disappeared to that had busted her chops to the top, earning an assignment with the special ops team? The one who would throat punch a man for an off comment just as quickly as she could staunch a gushing artery ripped open from enemy fire?

"Pease, Eena?" Carter batted his incredibly long lashes and leaned into her leg.

Oh, right. The big, warm eyes that reminded her of the color of moose hide and the sweet, squeaky voice that often spoke phrases that cut right to her steel heart had blown the woman she knew to smithereens. She hadn't wanted this assignment, but Zeke had insisted that the Rand boy needed an undercover bodyguard. Being the only woman on the Stryker Security Force qualified to protect the precious toddler made her the perfect one to play nanny. Or so Zeke said. Her insistence that the whole Manny thing was rising in popularity, and one of the guys could just as easily take the job, hadn't swayed Zeke's decision.

She should've tried harder.

"Okay, Carter." She sighed as she pulled him onto her lap, uncapped the marker, and flipped her notebook she'd been writing the morning's report in to a blank page.

She ran a hand over his downy hair as he scribbled on the paper. Over the last two months, Lena had found her carefully welded casing that she'd placed around her heart had chinks. A certain little boy had an uncanny way of seeping through the faults, softening her.

Making her weak.

She couldn't afford weakness ... vulnerability. She'd allowed that in once when she'd fallen in love with Ethan Stryker, the man who saw past her tough, Alaskan-bred exterior to the woman within who harbored hopes of finding a love like her parents had. The day he'd died, the hole in his chest as he'd lain lifeless on the helicopter deck had mirrored her own. When the fog of despair had lifted and she'd reluctantly come up for air, she'd started meticulously reinforcing the defenses around her shattered heart.

One look at Carter's blond hair that stuck up wildly like Ethan's had proved she hadn't worked hard enough at closing off her heart. Hadn't she already known that, though? Her time at Stryker had verified she still had feelings and could care, even though she wished she couldn't. Her need to push the soft-hearted Kiki and toughen her up had been more about Lena's own need to protect her friend than Kiki's desire to learn self-defense. Lena had to shield those powerless against life's travesties so they wouldn't end up wrecked like she had.

She glanced down the hall, anxious for Mr. Rand to get there. She'd be having a nice conversation with him about keeping her in the dark. She couldn't keep Carter safe if she didn't have all the intel, and from Mr. Rand's sharp tone, something had gone down.

Carter softly sang "Twinkle, Twinkle Little Star," the words skipping and getting jumbled as he tilted his head and scribbled away. Lena added her voice to his, causing him to peek back at her with a toothy smile. He returned to his drawing and sang with more gusto. Lena's mouth lifted slightly at the corners as she glanced around the living room of the rented townhome.

She shook her head and schooled her expression. She wasn't Carter's nanny. She couldn't forget protecting him remained her sole priority, even though the last two months she'd been here had the action of her mom's quilting circles —nothing but a bunch of gabbing and pointless work. Protecting the adorable child wasn't pointless, but she had seen no indication that this assignment was anything more than the inflated imaginings of a man with too much money to throw around—until today.

Marshall Rand didn't need her here twenty-four seven, practically sleeping in the same room with Carter the way the bathroom connected her room and the boy's. It wasn't like someone could sneak into the secure mansion back in Kentucky that the Rands lived in. Heck, even the town-home he'd rented for his trip to DC had enough security that she wasn't needed.

She still didn't understand why Mr. Rand had insisted that Carter, and therefore Lena, come with him to the capi-tol. He'd been wrapped up in so many meetings over the week that he hadn't come home until well after Carter's bedtime. She still could hear Mr. Rand's low comment that Carter went where he did, when she'd asked why the family was being dragged to Virginia.

Not that they were a family.

Far from it.

Though sometimes she wondered if what she experienced on the assignment was what most families' lives were like. The father leaving for work early in the morning. The kids doting on their fathers, never understanding why the man they admired most ran off each day instead of staying to play. The mother left with an aching loneliness that warred with accusing anger when left day after day to raise the kids with the husband coming in as the hero late in the night.

Lena shook her head. What a depressing thought and so unlike her own parents' marriage that she couldn't imagine being trapped in such a relationship. While it angered her when Mr. Rand came home too late to tuck Carter into bed, she had no say in how he ran his life. Which was fine by her.

If she'd known who the assignment was with in the first place, she probably would've told Zeke to find someone else. In fact, when she'd found out she'd be working for Marshall Rand, the ex-congressman who had flipped his vote on the bill that ultimately killed her fiancé, Ethan, she'd been ready to tell Zeke he had a week to find someone else. How could she possibly work for a man that could so carelessly leave soldiers ill-equipped?

How could she keep her disdain in when all she thought about was that spin in his moral compass that had been firmly pointing one way until the day of the vote?

She knew all about the bill that supposedly created

stronger borders, but only by making the troops in the field abroad weak with lack of support and proper equipment. She'd read the bill front to back, scoured the news and public documents associated with it, watched the debates, and researched all who had voted the bill through. The flip of Marshall Rand, and another congressman from Montana not showing up when the voting happened, had pushed the bill through. If Mr. Rand, uber-conservative representative and ex-Air Force member from Kentucky, would've just stuck to his guns, Ethan would still be alive. Lena would be married and probably have a child of her own sitting on her lap, scribbling indiscernible pictures while singing sweet songs.

Lena sat up straighter, horrified that her nose stung with unshed tears. She really should have followed through with telling Zeke to send someone else. Yet, she'd spent her days with Carter, and a week had tumbled into two that flowed to eight. She couldn't imagine being comfortable leaving his safety to anyone else, whether or not the risk was real.

Which meant she was more screwed than she wanted to acknowledge.

She glanced around the room at the toys scattered on the floor and the ragged teddy bear Carter hauled everywhere. Warmth spread through her as the morning fun rushed back to her. The joyful feeling brought an unease that started in her toes and inched up her body.

She couldn't do this anymore. Couldn't allow herself to be compromised again. Even being with Stryker Security had been a bad idea. She cared too much ... felt too much. When Mr. Rand finished schmoozing whoever it was he spent his days with, and they all returned to Kentucky, she would give General Paxton a call. He still needed people for his covert team bent on bringing down the organization responsible for the corruption that led to Ethan's death, the organization Stryker had too many run-ins with over the last year.

They were still trying to follow trails that connected June Rivas's mad dash across the country with Sosimo last fall with what Kiki's mom had disclosed after the entire fiasco in Colombia. There were so many threads to pull that Lena wondered if one of them, once untangled, would lead to Mr. Rand. Why else would he change his vote so suddenly? Maybe it was best for her to stick around and dig a little deeper.

"Eena, ook!" Carter leaned to the side and pointed at the scribbles that vaguely resembled bodies. "Me made us. At's you, me, and Daddy. We happy."

"That's nice, Carter." Lena squeezed the praise through her tight throat.

Who was she kidding? There wasn't enough evidence to suggest Rand was involved, and she couldn't stay on this assignment any longer. Not with the way her heart became entangled with Carter more and more with each passing day.

Instead of helping take down those who had killed Ethan and ruined her life, she helped the one who had betrayed his countrymen, giving up a piece of herself with each cheerful smile and heartwarming hug she received from Carter. Her warring emotions left her weary and on edge. Maybe she shouldn't wait until they returned to Kentucky. Maybe she should contact the general and set up an interview while they were here. Her heart picked up speed with the thought, and she couldn't tell if it was in anticipation or dread.

THREE

CARTER'S high-pitched singing accompanied by a lower, more beautiful voice greeted Marshall in the hallway to the living room. Even though he had a plan and had put it in motion, his heart still beat in his throat and his head buzzed with panic, so he leaned against the wall to calm himself. He didn't want to scare Carter. He also didn't want Lena Rebel to think he'd lost his cool. If her judgmental glances and low huffing were any indication, she already found him lacking. Flipping out like a crazed man would push any chance of gaining her respect right over the cliff.

Not that her thoughts toward him mattered. She might give everyone that look of deficiency for all he knew. It didn't change the fact that he came away from her presence feeling as if he'd failed ... again. He battled with that demon enough without her encouragement.

He took a deep breath, letting their song wash over him, and peeked into the room. Carter sat on Lena's lap at the small table against the window. She combed her fingers absentmindedly through his blond hair as she took in the surroundings. Carter's head bent over the table, his body wiggling side to side in a dance to the music. Man, how had Marshall's entire world gotten compressed into that one little body? There wouldn't be anything left of him if he lost Carter.

Lena shifted, her back straightening from its relaxed position. Even from the hallway, Marshall could see her jaw flex as she rapidly blinked her eyes. Was she trying not to cry? Marshall found it hard to believe she even had tender emotions.

"Eena, look." Carter turned on Lena's lap, his face bright with excitement as he explained the happy picture of the three of them together.

Like a family.

Jealousy scorched hot through his gut and raced heat to his face. Lena didn't deserve his son's love. She was nothing but a glorified babysitter. Carter should draw pictures of Amara, his mother, not some woman hired to watch him. *And whose fault is that?*

Marshall slumped against the wall, dragging his hand down his face. *My fault ... all mine.* Lena wasn't guilty of anything but doing her job. Carter was such a tender-hearted person, always loving, even to strangers. It made sense he'd include Lena in his affection. She'd been with him all hours of the day for the last two months.

"That's a beautiful picture." Lena's voice was tight, not her normal, efficient tone.

"Me made it for you." Carter pushed it into her hands.

The paper shook slightly as she took it. Why was a simple scribbling affecting her so much? Marshall never would've believed the tough-as-nails woman would get all mushy over such a thing. He'd known some resilient women from his time in the Air Force. Even his Amara had had an unbreakable attitude toward life, but he'd never met someone as focused and closed off as Lena Rebel.

"Thanks, buddy." She cleared her throat, her smile forced as she looked at Carter. "I'll keep it, even after I leave."

What did she mean by that?

Carter threw his little arms around her and kissed her soundly on the cheek. "Me love you, Eena."

Marshall couldn't take it anymore. Besides, they didn't have time to waste. He cleared his throat and stepped into the living room.

"Daddy!" Carter scrambled off of Lena's lap and rushed into Marshall's outstretched arms.

"Hey, squirt." Marshall tucked his head against Carter's, pulling his small body as close as he could.

Lena stood, her gaze bouncing down the hall before focusing like a laser to his face. Her expression had lost any softness it may have had while talking with Carter. Good. He needed her focused.

"What's wrong?" Her words clipped out like rapid-fire artillery, and her hand went to her concealed holster he knew she had tucked in the front of her jeans.

Good. Maybe her being all business all the time would come in handy finally.

"We need to leave now." Marshall stomped to the dinosaur backpack in the corner, carrying Carter with him.

"All right." Lena rushed to her pack he'd never seen her without and shoved her things in it. "What's going on?"

"I don't have time to explain right now." Marshall bent to pick up Carter's toys. "We leave in five. Can you be packed?"

Lena's eyes darted to the ceiling and back to Carter, still in Marshall's arms. It was irrational to still be holding him, but Marshall couldn't seem to force himself to put his son down. When she turned her gaze on Marshall, he lifted one brow in challenge.

"I've got him." Marshall put a hand on Carter's back in a move that bordered on possessive.

Lena must've picked up the sentiment because her forehead furrowed. She gave one quick nod, then hurried out of the room, taking the tension that had built out with her. Marshall let out a deep sigh, then focused on cramming as many toys as he could into the backpack.

"Where we going, Daddy?" Carter reached for his teddy bear and clutched it close. "Are we going home?"

Why had Marshall insisted Carter and Lena come with him? Had his meetings with legislators put his family back on the radar of whoever seemed to have such control? Maybe if he'd left Carter at home in Kentucky, whoever he'd upset would have just focused their pressure on Marshall. Then again, they might have gotten to Carter easier back home.

Marshall shook his head. At least with him here, Marshall wouldn't have the plane ride home to spend filled with worry over what he'd find when he got home.

"We're going on a trip to a great enormous lake." Marshall set Carter down so he could zip up the backpack.

Carter clapped and did a little dance from side to side. "Me love lakes."

A small smile pushed Marshall's cheeks up as he breathed a quick laugh out of his nose. Even when his blood pressure was about to soar to the sky with stress, this kid lightened his mood.

"What's the plan?" Lena stomped in, her and Carter's duffels packed.

He glanced at his watch. Three minutes. Impressive.

"We're heading to the airport, then leaving for a private location." Marshall picked Carter back up, the command in his voice sharp. "Security detail only."

One delicate eyebrow rose over her dark, almost black eyes. "Okay." She nodded to Carter. "If we're keeping the premise that I'm just a nanny, I'll need to take him."

Marshall squeezed Carter tighter. His son looked from Lena to Marshall, his head tilting to the side in confusion. Just when Marshall had gotten his heart rate under control, it picked back up. A tightness banded across his chest as he shifted from one foot to the other.

Lena's eyes softened a moment. Her cheek flexed, and the expression disappeared. Placing the bags on the carpet, she stepped close and opened her hands in a non-combative move.

"If my assignment has changed, I can fall in formation with the rest of your detail." She took another step closer. "But if you want my position as bodyguard to stay on the down low, I need to appear like who you've set me up to be."

It made sense. Not even Ed knew her actual identity. To everyone but Marshall, she was Elena Anderson, Carter's nanny.

When he'd approached Zeke Greene, owner of Stryker Security Force, the ex-special force member had insisted that no one know what Lena was there for. Her assignment would be compromised if her true purpose wasn't kept undercover. Since his friend and business associate, June Rivas, insisted Stryker was the best, Marshall agreed to Zeke's terms.

It didn't make letting his son go into the arms of another any easier. He swallowed, patted Carter on the back, and handed him to her. Then, without looking back, he stepped past and grabbed the bags from where she'd dropped them.

As he led them down the hall and to the waiting car, his mind raced with what still needed to be done. How could he leave and risk everything he'd pushed for the last months to fall apart? What if Ed wasn't able to talk the remaining waffling legislators into signing the bill limiting terms?

Lena buckled Carter into his carseat as he bounced his teddy on his lap and sang a nonsense song about lakes. She smiled at him, but her eyes scanned behind them through the back window of the car. The movement wasn't obvious, and if Marshall didn't know why she was really with their family, he wouldn't have noticed.

"Daddy?" Carter gazed up at him, drawing his attention. "We see fish in the lake?"

"Maybe." Marshall swallowed as Carter's face lit up just like Amara's used to.

"Me loves fish." He squeezed his teddy into a hug.

"Me too, buddy." Marshall stared at his son.

His worries over the upcoming bill faded to a low buzz at the back of his brain as the car sped toward the airport. Even the demands of his manufacturing business slowed their constant whirl within his brain. Nothing mattered above his son's safety. There would always be another chance to support new laws if there weren't enough votes to get the change the nation needed this time. Even the expansions for the company in Texas could wait until things settled. First, he'd get Carter secure, then see what needed done next.

FOUR

LENA STARED out the wall-to-ceiling windows at Lake Coeur d'Alene in northern Idaho as she stalked to Mr. Rand's office. She had to admit the scenery took her breath away. Though, as beautiful as it was, it couldn't compare to her Alaskan mountains.

They'd arrived late the night before after racing to the airport and hopscotching across the nation. Ed had been waiting on the small airport's tarmac, and he and Mr. Rand had whispered low before Mr. Rand had clapped Ed on the shoulder. Ed had lingered in the hug he'd given Carter, the corner of his eyes crinkled in concern. Something big had happened, and even though Mr. Rand had many opportunities to explain, she still had limited intel, which caused her muscles to twitch in anticipation of the unknown.

That would change in about two-point-three seconds, whether or not Mr. Rand was ready to spew. Lena flexed her fingers, the snapping sound reminding her to relax. Her ma had always said Lena was too quick to push her objectives, insisting she'd get people to see her way if she used a chisel instead of a wrecking ball. Lena had chiseled away the day before and all morning with questioning looks and pointed statements. With Carter taking a nap, it was past time to call in the heavy equipment.

Her phone buzzed in her pocket, startling her to a stop. She hadn't left it in the plane like Mr. Rand had insisted all the security detail, even himself, do. Rafe had put so much protection on her phone, there would be no way for anyone to track it, and she needed a secure way to contact the team. Since taking this assignment, she hadn't talked with anyone but her weekly check-in with Zeke and the monthly calls to her ma. Everyone knew she hated being bothered while working.

She pulled out the phone and rolled her eyes when her brother's picture smiled up at her. Bjørn always was the first to push her buttons. He was also her closest sibling. Surviving war together would do that.

"What?" Lena huffed into the phone as she scanned the lake's shore.

"Wow, Lena, it's so nice to talk to you too." Bjørn's exaggerated cheerfulness had her eyes heading toward the back of her lids again.

She shook her head to stop the childish motion. Her nerves made her snarky—well, snarkier than normal. Her brother didn't deserve her ire.

"Sorry. It's been a trying day." She took a calming breath while she watched a pair of ducks glide across the lake's surface.

"What? A toddler's too much for you to handle? Do you need reinforcements?" Bjørn snickered, and her eyes narrowed.

What was she thinking when she told him the basics of this job? *Note to self: cut Bjørn off of inside information and beat him to a pulp at the next possible opportunity.* She smiled at the thought of their next sparring round. She'd make sure he paid.

"All right. Unless you have a reason for calling, I'm hanging up." Lena glanced down the hall, then checked the video feed of Carter that streamed to her watch.

Having a rich boss had its advantages. Her watch would beep and vibrate on her wrist when it detected movement in the room. Perfect for watching out for intruders and keeping tabs on a little boy who liked to sneak out of his room and find himself a snack.

"I wanted you to know that I finally found her." Bjørn's excitement pulled at her through the phone, and she was suddenly glad for the chance to talk to him.

"You mean you finally got someone to date you?" Lena smirked at her own joke, then went in for the kill. "Did Ma have to set you up again?"

"No, Lena, my bird. I finally found the perfect helicopter." He made a noise that bordered on a snort. "And, I'll have you know, I have no problem finding dates on my own."

With his handsome looks and daring personality, she doubted he had any trouble at all. Which made her wonder why he hadn't found someone in the last year since he'd been out of the military? For that matter, why hadn't he dated much while in the military?

"Is she everything you ever wanted?" Lena teased.

"And more. This beaut has all the whistles. I'll be able to use it guiding, search and rescue, air tours, you name it."

She could picture him flying over the Alaskan Range, the midnight sun shining brightly through the windshield. The longing for home hit her hard and fast, like a perfectly aimed right hook to the solar plexus. She closed her eyes, willing the emotion to leave.

She cleared her throat and forced her words out. "That sounds amazing."

Bjørn continued like he didn't notice the thickness in her voice. Which didn't surprise her. She knew how he could get tunnel vision. It seemed to be a family trait, whether good or bad.

"I'm in Spokane picking her up right now." The distinct *ch-ch* of a helicopter sounded in the background.

"Spokane? When do you leave?"

He was only about thirty minutes away. The need to see family burned so hot she almost told him where she was. Could she get a few hours off to run and see him? She shook her head.

Don't be a ninny.

She didn't know why Mr. Rand had raced them across the country. If it was half as bad as he made it out to be, then she wouldn't be seeing her family or anyone else for a while. She really needed to go talk to him and figure out what was going on.

"I'm flying out tomorrow, probably early afternoon. I need to do a few things before I leave, make sure she's ready for the long trip. Plan on hopping her home to the parents' in time for the anniversary party." His words sank heavy to the bottom of her stomach.

She'd forgotten all about her parents' thirty-fifth anniversary. They'd be having a big shindig at the ranch with all the siblings, aunts and uncles, and cousins. She hadn't been to a gathering in so long, she wondered if she'd even recognize anyone.

"I'm thrilled for you, Bjørn." Lena bit her lip, ready to finish with this call so she could get back to work, but also hating not keeping this reminder of home on the phone a little longer. "I'll be praying for your trip. Let me know when you make it, okay?"

"Will do, but only if you promise to answer the phone with a smile. You've been cranky as a bear lately." He grunted like a grizzly at a bait stand, then laughed. "Love you, Lena. Stay safe."

"Love you too." She stared at the phone as the call ended and the screen turned black.

Yeah, well, he'd be cranky, too, if he was doing this job. She shoved the phone in her pocket at the lie she was trying to sell herself. The job, though not as dangerous as some of her others, wasn't so bad. That was, when she didn't want to strangle her boss. She'd miss Carter more than she cared to admit when this assignment was over.

She scanned the scenery one last time, cocking her head when she spied Tony at the edge of the yard. He had his wrist up to his mouth, his lips moving. Oh, to be able to go outside and patrol the grounds like Tony and the other guards did. She'd even take the night shift. It'd feel more normal than the nanny business.

She stepped toward Mr. Rand's office with a huff. She might not feel like a glorified babysitter if she had a clue what was going on. Her boss's evasion was over.

As she approached the open doorway with determination, her hand poised to knock on the frame, she saw him and froze. Marshall Rand stood at the window, his strong shoulders drooped and eyes glassy as he stared across the lake. Grief and regret filled the room, almost pushing her back. He rubbed his hand across his chest like it ached.

She knew that feeling and clenched her fingers so she wouldn't touch her own. How could her chest still hurt even though it was empty? It had been two years since Ethan had died. Shouldn't the pain fade, or was she doomed to live with it forever?

"Oh, Amara." Mr. Rand dropped his chin to his chest with a heavy sigh. "What am I going to do?"

The heaviness in his voice twinged something in her she didn't understand. Was it empathy? Maybe guilt for being such a jerk to him since she got here. She shook her head and took a step back. She had every reason to not like Mr. Rand. He'd ruined her life, after all. She'd do her job and protect Carter, but that didn't mean she had to like his father.

Stepping backward, she planned a retreat. She'd let him sulk in whatever misery he probably deserved. Her stomach soured at the merciless thought. When had her heart turned so black? No one deserved that.

She inched back another step, hoping Mr. Rand wouldn't notice her. She had to get out of there. Her skin turned clammy as her pulse picked up. She'd just call Zeke, tell him to find someone else to take this position ASAP.

Her watch beeped and vibrated, jerking her to a stop. Carter rolled over in his bed, clutching his teddy to his chest and releasing Lena's breath that had bottled up in her chest. She glanced up, and her gaze collided with the dark blue of Mr. Rand's. She should have snuck away when she could.

FIVE

MARSHALL MARVELED as Lena Rebel's expression warred with emotion. It was the first time in two months that something other than disdain or flat-out dismissal had crossed her face when in his presence. He knew she had other emotions. He'd witnessed them when he'd spied on her with Carter. Well, not spied, rather supervised. What played across her face now resembled doubt and maybe guilt.

Lena Rebel didn't doubt. At least, not that he'd seen. And she'd definitely never expressed remorse around him. Just what had she seen in his expression to cause the unflappable woman to flutter? He turned fully to her, not wanting to think about his perceived weakness.

"Something wrong? Why aren't you with Carter?" He used his big boss voice, hoping she'd just leave him in peace to grieve over his failures.

Lena's beautiful eyes flashed, and a shiver of awareness raced down Marshall's spine. He shifted, not comprehending if the reaction was in fear or excitement. His pulse beat like a duck's wings before taking off—fast and violent.

Excitement couldn't be right. She despised him, and he hadn't been attracted to anyone since Amara. Never would. So, it must be fear, though the buzz running through him felt nothing like any fear he'd experienced before.

"Carter's fine. You're the one acting like a ground squirrel when the grizzlies come hunting." Lena stepped into the room and the buzzing skimming along Marshall's skin intensified and made it hard to concentrate.

"Did you just call me a squirrel?" Marshall crossed his arms over his chest to ease the discomfort her presence brought.

"Yes. You're acting squirrelly, and I need to know why." She stopped with her feet planted wide, and one perfect brow raised above her dark brown, almost black, eye.

"Why?" Marshall parroted, and Lena's eyes rolled.

After all this time, why did his brain have to go and decide it found Lena Rebel, of all people, attractive? She was the exact opposite of his tenderhearted Amara. Where she was light and vivacious, Lena was hard and callous, unless she interacted with Carter. Her sharp tongue and steely demeanor melted away around his son. The memory of her lyrical voice singing along with Carter's sent another shiver down his back. This wouldn't do. Wouldn't do at all.

"Yes, why." She sat in the chair in front of his desk and muttered below her breath, "I thought he was supposed to be smart." Her quiet comment wasn't soft enough to escape his notice and shook him out of his stupor. He moved to his seat behind the desk as she continued. "Why are we holed up on the far side of Lake Coeur d'Alene? What made you drop everything and run scared?"

He sat up straighter as heat filled his chest. He wasn't running scared. His leaving was well calculated, especially until he could assess the extent of the danger.

"Yesterday, while at lunch with an investor, I received a message." Fear chilled his defensive anger just thinking of those words.

"A Facebook message from a jilted lover? An invitation to go fishing with a long-lost friend?" Lena motioned to the lake outside, her increasing annoyance evident in her voice. "Don't be obtuse, Mr. Rand."

He stifled the grin that threatened at her sharp words. People rarely challenged him anymore, especially employees. When they did, it wasn't so upfront and in his face. He liked it, more than he cared to admit.

"Read for yourself." He pulled the receipt from his back pocket and tossed it across his desk.

As her eyes scanned the words, her light brown skin paled.

"The only lover I've ever had is buried back home in Kentucky." Marshall swallowed the grief always skimming under the surface. "I won't let that happen to the other half of my heart."

Lena lifted her gaze to his, and he was shocked to find regret there. Fiery passion pushed the regret away as her chin hardened.

"They won't hurt Carter." Purpose and a promise laced her voice. "As long as I'm alive."

They stared at each other across the desk, a sense of camaraderie stretching between them. They may not know each other well. Her underhanded disapproval got on his nerves, and it was obvious she didn't like him very much. They both loved Carter, though, and that was more than enough to bind them together to keep him safe. Lena shifted and broke their connection by glancing back at the receipt.

"'Do what we say.' What is it they want?" She tossed the paper back toward him.

"About ten minutes after they slipped me this, I received a text on my private line demanding I stop supplying your friend June with materials for her inventions and that I forget about my push for term limits in the legislature." He sighed, grabbed the note, meticulously folding it into a square, and placed it back in his pocket. "Basically, stop everything I'm doing or else."

"That's what you've been doing in DC?" Lena's face scrunched in confusion. "But you're no longer in Congress."

"That doesn't mean I don't want to see change." His ego ruffled. He was getting sick of how every word she said caused his defenses to rise. "My term in Congress showed me how having lifetime appointments has denigrated our system, allowing corruption and money to influence lawmaking rather than the good of the people. If lawmakers only had a limited time in the capitol, then maybe they'd spend less time stuffing bills to appease their money masters and more time representing the people who elected them."

Marshall blew out a frustrated huff as Lena's eyes widened. Why did he always have to get so riled up? He needed to learn how to respond without calling on his best *Braveheart* persona.

"Sorry." He shrugged, laughing at himself. "I get a little passionate."

"If this is how you feel, why'd you get out after only one term? Why not stay longer to push change from the inside?"

Maybe she'd stop shooting daggers his way if she understood him better. He shook his head. He obviously needed a vacation, a retreat, something. His mind hadn't been this distracted since college. How could he answer without telling the whole truth and exposing his own treason to the citizens he'd sworn to protect?

"After Amara's murder, I inherited her family's company." He ran his hands along the smooth wood desktop. "I couldn't do that, raise Carter, and fulfill my congressional duties."

"I don't remember her death being a murder." Lena's voice softened, almost like she was shifting blocks of knowledge in her brain so they'd fit right.

"Officially, it wasn't. She died in a car crash." He should have told Zeke that info when Marshall had contacted Stryker for security, but he'd kept the reason for his need for a bodyguard general. Shame had a way of piling secrets.

Marshall fisted his hand on the desk so he wouldn't reach into his pocket to finger the paper he'd torn from his wife's journal. The letter his dear Amara had sent from the grave, detailing the intimidation she'd been under to convince him to vote for the border bill. She'd begged him to forgive her, that she'd only been thinking of Carter, though she knew the bill had issues neither of them agreed with. He'd found the page a week after the bill passed, his yes vote in honor of his deceased wife sealing it into law. In a need to be closer to her, he'd read her journal only to find that his flipping his support for the bill he questioned wasn't for her, but for some unknown organization that had leveraged Carter for her cooperation. He had kept the paper in his pocket, rereading it anytime he questioned what needed done, so he'd never forget the price of failure again.

His gaze connected with Lena's. "But from that threat, it's obvious my wife's crash was no accident."

Lena didn't have to know that he'd figured that out two years ago. All she needed to know was that the threat was real, and that her job had just gotten more intense. His leg bounced with the need for action, the need to fix this before it escalated too high for him to contain.

"I wonder if it's the same group that attacked June last

fall?" Lena bit her bottom lip in concentration. "I'll contact my team and see what they can find out. Maybe digging into your threats might be what's needed to blow this whole thing apart." Lena's watch beeped, causing her to glance at it and stand. "Carter's up."

She stopped and stared at Marshall. Her gaze bounced between his eyes like she searched for something. Finally, she wetted her lips and swallowed. "Maybe you should come play with him for a while. Since we're here just hanging out, it might be a good opportunity to get some quality time in with him."

He nodded, his throat tight with the implication he didn't know his son like he should. With the invitation issued, she spun on her heel and marched out of the room. Marshall stared after her until she turned the corner, then he stared at the empty wall as he stuffed whatever attraction he felt for her in a mental box and locked it tight.

It wasn't *her*, per se, which drew him, though there was no denying she was drop-dead gorgeous. It was the stress of the situation and her affection for Carter that had his mind zinging. It was his stupidity to come to this town that had been his and Amara's first vacation together that had his heart pounding in his chest. He had let the fear of the threat control his emotions and distract him from his focus. It didn't mean there was actually anything to his sudden pull to Lena.

Just so his brain never forgot what happened when he didn't stay sharp, he pulled out Amara's journal page from his pocket. She'd sacrificed so much to protect their son, and he hadn't even noticed. The words burned in his heart, searing it anew with a call to action. With his purpose fully restored to the forefront of his mind, he strode down the hall to bond with his son.

SIX

MARSHALL SQUEEZED Carter's hand as they trekked through the city park back to the vehicle. He was glad he'd made the security team leave their phones on the plane and left the pilot with explicit instructions to continue his zigzag across the nation. Because of that, Marshall was confident that a trip into town so Carter could ride the historic carousel would be fine. They had let Carter play on the Fort Sherman Playground, done two rounds on the carousel— since Carter had two favorite horsies and he didn't want to hurt their feelings—and now they sipped on the fresh-squeezed lemonades they'd gotten from a vendor as they meandered down the shaded sidewalk.

"Me love going round and round." Carter jumped, pulling on Marshall's hand. "Me love horsies."

He neighed and galloped around Marshall and Lena in a figure eight, the backpack he'd insisted on wearing bumbling against his back. It had annoyed Marshall at first that Carter wanted to wear his pack everywhere like Lena did. Wasn't a boy supposed to want to be like his daddy? Carter couldn't copy anything of Marshall's but his hurried conversations and quick kisses. He wanted to change that, which made this time even more important to him.

He glanced around, the presence of his three other bodyguards helping him relax even more into the experience. When was the last time he'd taken Carter out to have fun? Marshall couldn't remember, and the fact sank hard into his gut. No wonder Lena looked at him with such contempt.

That would change too. He'd lain awake long into the night thinking about his relationship, or lack of, with his son. He would never honor Amara's sacrifice if their son barely knew him. He didn't have to be everywhere at all times. That's what he had Ed for. Marshall needed to loosen the reins a bit and delegate more. Ed could handle it —would relish it, actually. This time of limited communication would be the perfect test of just how well Ed could run things.

A man stepped out from the bushes that lined the sidewalk, pulling Marshall's attention back to the present. He looked like every other person they'd encountered that day, wearing shorts and a T-shirt, and carrying an ice cream in his hand. Something about the way the guy eyed the bodyguard leading the way caused the hair on Marshall's scalp to rise. He snagged Carter's hand as he galloped by. Lena's sucked breath shot Marshall's gaze to her, where Tony, the head of Marshall's security, held a gun against her side.

"Did you honestly think you could escape, Mr. Rand?" Tony smirked, condescension thick in his tone. "Running will only bring more trouble."

Marshall pulled Carter against him as his gaze darted to Lena's. He followed hers as it jumped from the man from the bushes, now pointing a gun at the other bodyguard, and the mirror situation with the third guard that had been trailing behind. At least there was just one traitor among them and not all of them. Marshall returned his attention to Tony and Lena, and stifled his surprise when she winked. She had a plan, and he needed to be ready to act. Four years in the Air Force hadn't been for nothing, even if he had been just an analyst.

"Please, I'll do whatever you want, just let Carter and Elena go." Marshall put as much pleading in his voice as he could stomach, hoping to buy Lena some time.

"Daddy?" Carter looked up at Marshall, confusion on his small face.

"You lost that chance when you decided to run." Tony tightened his grip on Lena's arm. "There's someone who wants to chat."

Lena exploded, her arm swinging up and nailing Tony in the Adam's apple. His eyes bulged as he dropped his gun and clutched his throat. The other two guards followed Lena's lead and attacked. Marshall lifted Carter into his arms, holding him tightly.

Lena took off through the park, grabbing Marshall's arm as she passed, and jerked him with her. He stretched his legs to keep up with her, his daily five-mile run paying off. Carter whimpered against Marshall's neck and wrapped his tiny arms so tightly Marshall worried he'd choke. Lena dashed just ahead of him, her hand poised over her side where she probably concealed her sidearm. She seemed to know exactly where she was heading, so he kept his focus on planting his feet and holding Carter close. He chanced a glance behind him just as the guy who had stepped into their path burst from the bushes, spotting them an instant later.

"Lena, they're coming." Marshall pushed harder, willing his legs to move faster.

They emerged from the trees into a parking lot. His harsh breaths and the slapping of their feet on the pavement thundered in his ears. Where was she taking them?

"Marshall, get ahead of me." No strain or exhaustion was apparent in her voice as she slowed just enough for him to pass her. "Keep going. Straight ahead, through those trees."

He aimed for the trees, hoping refuge waited on the other side. His lungs burned. He obviously had been taking his runs too easy.

The pop of a small caliber gun caused him to duck and tuck Carter in front of him. Why were they shooting? He couldn't chat if he was dead. The fear that adrenaline had pushed out of his brain skated back up his spine.

Lena grunted behind him. Had they shot her? He peeked back just as she spun and took out their pursuers with two clean shots. A thrill of excitement tingled and twisted along the fear. This was insane ... and exhilarating.

He crashed into the trees, covering Carter's head against the limbs. They emerged at a busy intersection just as the crossing signal beeped. How had she known this was here?

"Go. Cross the street. Don't stop." She nudged his back, and he dashed across the street.

The light changed, and the waiting cars honked as they raced pass. When they reached the opposite side, he peeked back to see Tony glaring across the busy traffic, his phone to his ear. He'd been on Marshall's security detail for over three years. How long had the man been an enemy?

Lena's head whipped back to look behind them. "We have to hurry." Rushing to a beat-up single-cab pickup, she jerked the driver's door open and motioned for them to get in. He scooted across the bench seat, pushing empty fast-food trash aside and climbing over a toolbox.

"Get on the floorboard and stay down." Lena tossed her backpack onto the bench. "I need you to get my hat out of there."

He tucked Carter underneath him and scrunched onto the floorboard. There was barely enough room for them both to fit. He adjusted his legs, trying to get more comfortable, then reached for her bag.

She grabbed the toolbox on the seat, rifling through the contents and pulling out a screwdriver and hammer. What did she plan to do? She placed the screwdriver in the ignition. There was no way she could hot wire the truck. Shouldn't they keep running, maybe look for a cop or something? Marshall pulled out her hat and set it next to her, doubt clinging to his throat as he tried to catch his breath.

"Daddy, me scared." Carter trembled under him, curling his little body against Marshall's.

"Hey, squirt. It's okay." He rubbed his hand over his son's curls. "We're not letting anything happen to you."

A loud metallic whack jerked Marshall's head up just in time to watch Lena slam the hammer a second time against the screwdriver's handle. She turned the tool jutting from the steering column, and the truck fired to life. Where in the world did she learn that? He was pretty sure they didn't teach that in the army.

"I'm giving you a raise," he blurted out over the loud country blaring through the speakers.

Her lips tweaked in the most adorable way as she twisted the volume down. If she knew he'd just thought that, she'd probably throat chop him like she had Tony. She ripped off her T-shirt, revealing a white tank top underneath, yanked her hair tie from her ponytail to let her long raven hair spill down her back, and slammed the hat on her head.

"You might want to wait on that raise." She threw the truck in gear and sped out of the parking lot. "I haven't gotten us to safety yet."

The words sobered the amazement coursing through him. How did she plan to do that? She took a turn, and Marshall grunted as he slammed against the door. His five-ten frame was not meant to fold into such a compact space. Lena's gaze darted to him, then back to the road.

"Strip."

"Excuse me?" He stuttered.

"You have the Supersuit Zeke gave you on under your polo, right?"

"Yeah."

"Then strip out of your polo and get on the seat. Changing your shirt will help disguise you." She glanced at the side mirror. "I need you up and watching for a tail."

He set the toolbox on the floorboard and clambered onto the bench seat. Then he tucked Carter onto his feet. Was it safe for him to be on the floorboard like that? It'd be better if he was in a seatbelt. He pulled Carter onto the middle spot on the bench seat and buckled his son in.

Marshall then tore off his polo, the button catching in his hair and ripping a chunk out. He cringed as he remembered the Captain America shirt he had on over the formfitting suit, glad he'd put that on but also wishing he'd chosen something less childish. He never imagined anyone would actually see the shirt he wore as a boost to his ego. Not that his embarrassment mattered at the moment.

"Hey, buddy. Why don't you lay your head on my lap for a while?" Marshall rubbed his son's small shoulder and eased him to his lap.

What else could he do to help? He grabbed the knitted beanie stuffed in the dashboard's corner. It smelled of sweat and dirt, but if Lena said they needed a disguise, he'd follow suit. He put the sunglasses on that had been next to the beanie and turned to her.

"What do you need me to do?"

"Watch the mirror. If you see someone continually taking the same turns as us, let me know." She pulled out her phone, the screen coming to life.

Marshall growled. "Did anyone listen to me about leaving their phones?"

Lena rolled her eyes. "Oh, thank God you haven't left yet." The relief in her voice was unexpected as she slid the phone in the holder clipped to the truck's vents and turned on the speaker.

Just who was she talking to?

"You missed me that much?" The cocky tone grated on Marshall's already fraying nerves.

He watched in the mirror as she took a turn, scanning the scant cars behind, his ribs seeming too tight as his breathing slowed. He was ill-equipped for this. He should have done more training instead of relying on others to protect him. All he knew about watching for tails he learned through movies. He doubted his lessons were thorough enough for the nightmare they were now in.

"I'm heading your way. We need an escape that's off the books." Lena turned down another side street.

"What happened?" The man's arrogant voice turned to steel.

"I'll fill you in when we're in the air. Text me the address. We'll be there in less than thirty, and you better be ready to take off."

"Dang it, Len—"

She disconnected the phone and peeked at Carter before pulling her gaze up to Marshall's. "See anything back there?"

Marshall peered behind them one more time before shaking his head. "No. At least, I don't think so. Everything I know about enemy evasion, I learned from Jason Bourne."

Lena laughed as she turned from Hastings Avenue to 15th Street. The sound tinkled in his ears and skittered along his skin. Had he ever heard her laugh before? Maybe, but never in a way that sounded so unguarded. She stopped at a red light, scanning all three mirrors and surrounding vehicles before her eyes slid to Carter.

"He fell asleep?" Lena's soft expression captivated Marshall as she slid her hand down Carter's arm and curled her fingers around his hand.

How had he thought she was void of emotion? Why did she hide behind the wall of aggravation when she was with him? But, more importantly, why did it suddenly matter so much to Marshall that her reactions to him change?

"I'll get us out of this, Marshall." His name on her lips spread warmth through his stomach like he'd just taken a shot of espresso. "I promise. I won't let anything happen to him."

"Thank you, Lena," he whispered past the lump in his throat and set his hand over hers that still held Carter's.

She looked at their hands, her eyebrows squishing together the way Carter's did when he was confused. He wished he could read minds to know if her heart was racing as fast as his. It was probably just the adrenaline still coursing through him. She swallowed, pulled her hand free, and focused on the road as the light turned green.

The interstate loomed before them, and Marshall's

growing respect for Lena doubled. "How did you know where to go?"

"I studied a map of the town before we left and memorized exit plans." Lena shrugged like escaping murderous traitors was an everyday event.

"You're amazing." He couldn't keep the awe from his voice.

"No, just paranoid."

She took the interstate west, pulling in between two minivans like they were just another family heading somewhere for the weekend. The steady hum of the tires speeding along the pavement eased the tension bunched in his muscles, and he gripped Carter's hand in his own. She may chalk it up to paranoia, but hiring Lena Rebel may have been the best decision Marshall had ever made.

SEVEN

MAKING this job personal may have been the stupidest thing Lena had ever done. She breathed deeply through her nose to calm her still racing heart. She peeked at Carter sleeping peacefully on Marshall's leg, and her pulse ratcheted right back up. What if she wasn't good enough? What if she made a mistake that got Carter killed?

As the what-ifs wrapped fear tighter and tighter around her chest, doubt clouded her thoughts and made it hard to think straight. Why had she ever thought she could take this solo assignment? She couldn't wait to get to Bjørn and get in the air. Maybe when there were ten thousand feet between them and their attackers, she could stop freaking out.

She turned into the dirt drive her phone indicated and pulled up to the metal hangar at the end of a private runway. Bjørn stepped from the building with another man and lifted his hand in greeting as he dashed to the helicopter and tossed in his pack. Her chest eased at the sight of him, and the relief pinched her pride.

She had trained hard for half of her life, if not more, for situations like what they had just gone through. She shouldn't need anyone else. If she was good enough, she could do this on her own. But she wasn't, and she didn't know where that left her.

She threw the truck into park and turned the screwdriver to kill the engine. "Come on. Let's get in the helo." She opened her door but paused as she took in the huge lumberjack of a man with her brother. "Stay behind me until I assess the situation, okay?"

Marshall's eyes widened as they bounced to the guys approaching the truck. "I thought you knew them."

"I do, well, one of them." She sighed. "Remember, I'm paranoid."

She tried to make the comment light by adding a smile, but she feared it came off as more of a grimace. Snagging her pack and jumping from the truck, she hurried around the hood so she'd be in front of Marshall and Carter in case the worst happened. Her brother ruined her cautious plans when he raced up and grabbed her into a hug. She squeezed her eyes shut, relishing the physical connection that filled her tank that she wasn't aware was bone-dry.

"Lena." Bjørn set her down and grabbed her shoulders, shaking her. "Are you kidding me? Do you know what I've been going through the last half hour?"

Her lip twitched up at the reprimand. "Sorry about that. I had to focus."

Movement caught her eye behind Bjørn, and she straightened. How had she let her guard slip again? She had done it in the park when Carter's joy had distracted her and allowed Tony to get the drop on her. Now she'd done it again with her brother's welcome. Why was it so hard for her to keep her emotions under control? She'd never had this problem before, not even on the mission that killed Ethan.

Bjørn pointed his thumb over his shoulder. "You remember Tank from the Night Stalkers?"

Tank? As in Zac "the Tank" Smith who flew with Bjørn in the 160th SOAR for the army? She didn't recognize him with his face covered in a thick, unruly beard and his long hair pulled back in a man bun. Lena hardly had time for the information to process before Bjørn was blazing forward.

"Hey, I'm Bjørn. Looks like I'm going to be your captain today." Bjørn nodded at Marshall, still behind Lena. She snapped back to what needed done.

"Right." She motioned to the Rands, pausing at the pinched expression on Marshall's face. "Mr. Rand, this is my brother, Bjørn, and our friend Zac. Guys, that's Mr. Rand and Carter."

"It's Marshall." His face relaxed as he nodded, then fixed his gaze on Lena. "Just Marshall."

Her chest heated, and she furrowed her forehead. Why was he suddenly informal? And when had she started thinking of him as Marshall? If she didn't move this reunion along, her entire face might break out in a sweat. She had no reason to flush over Mr. Rand and his confusing expressions. Both of their emotions were running high on adrenaline at the moment, which meant she couldn't put meaning into anything either of them did.

She pushed everything down but her irritation. That, she knew and was comfortable with. "Are you ready to go or what?"

"Bossy, bossy." Bjørn chuckled as he motioned to the helicopter. "We're ready. Just waiting on you."

"We were here hiding out and were found." Lena pointed behind her with her thumb in a move that mirrored Bjørn's at the truck. Man, she'd missed being with family. "I had to borrow a truck."

"She hotwired it with a screwdriver and a hammer." Marshall's awestruck voice slid like melted dark chocolate down her ragged insides. "She was amazing. I've never seen anything like what she did back there."

"She's a keeper for sure." Bjørn's smirk made Lena want to deck him. "Aren't you glad I taught you how to do that all those years ago?"

"You taught me?" She rolled her eyes at the memory of their camping trip when Bjørn had somehow lost the keys to the truck and their father had had to start the vehicle like she had. She turned to Tank. "I'm really sorry to dump this all on you, but we need the truck to be wiped clean of any evidence of us being in it."

He shrugged. "That won't be a problem. I'll make sure it's clean before I park it somewhere."

She pulled her phone out of her pocket and clicked on the app Rafe had installed that ran a kill code, erasing everything on the phone. She couldn't take any chances that the phone had somehow been traced. She typed in the passcode, set the phone so it wouldn't lock up, and handed it to Tank.

"Is it possible for you to take this down the road a bit?" She rubbed the back of her neck. "If they somehow traced it, I don't want them coming here and bothering you."

"Got it."

"Just click on that execute button and the phone will wipe clean."

He nodded and pulled her into a hug she wasn't expecting. "Stay safe."

Her throat closed with stupid, unshed tears, so she jerked her head in acknowledgment. She had to get herself under control. Had to get safely in the air so she could just breathe and lock everything that threatened to burst from her back into its rightful place. She'd let her feelings lead her once before and look where that got her—with a dead fiancé and a shattered heart. Hadn't she learned her lesson?

She stomped after her brother, who was leading the Rands. Carter skipped next to his dad with Marshall clinging to his hand. The cute kid glanced back to her with such excitement shining from his face that her heart melted all over again. How would she ever put herself back together if she stayed with Carter?

If she didn't, what other feelings would sneak in and bombard her heart?

Her eyes flicked to Marshall as the memory of his touch on her hand rushed back. The sparks that had shot up her arm had left her with a sick feeling in the pit of her stomach. Problem was, she couldn't tell if it was revulsion or attraction. It had to be the former. She wasn't attracted to him. Well, she shouldn't be attracted to him. He'd been part of what led to Ethan's death. On top of that, he piecemealed his time and love out to his son like some fiendish guard at a concentration camp. The poor boy starved for his daddy's attention, but never got enough moments to truly satisfy his hunger.

Her jaw ached as she clenched her teeth at the well-known bitterness that welled within her. She just had to keep all that fresh in her mind until she contained this situation and she could get another assignment. If she had any hope of pulling herself back to where she'd been comfortable, she'd have to distance herself emotionally from Carter.

"Come on, Eena." Carter ran up and tugged on her hand, the motion wrenching open the chinks around her heart even further. "Me going on a elicoper."

His big brown eyes, filled with such trust and love, beamed up at her. How could she cut herself off from the person who meant so much to her? Her indecision during the attack and the panic that had filled her threatened to fray her senses again. When his safety was on the line, how could she wall herself up so she could protect him better? It had everything to do with keeping him safe, and nothing to do with the confusing emotions churning within her. She helped Carter climb into the helicopter and swallowed the bitter lie.

EIGHT

"ZEKE, IT'S LENA." Lena sat on the edge of the hotel's bed as the call connected to the secure line back home, exhaustion weighing her muscles down.

After much arguing, she'd agreed to Bjørn's insistence that they take the Rands to Alaska, and they had spent the next eight hours flying over the Canadian forest. The excitement of the flight had kept Carter entertained for the first leg, but each one after became harder for the child to stay happy. Lena was glad she wasn't a real nanny. Cranky kids were not her cup of tea.

"What's wrong?" Zeke's question shot through the phone like he'd never left the military, quick and efficient.

"Marshall's head of security ended up being in with the people pressuring him." Lena hadn't meant for his first name to slip out, wanting to keep things between them formal, but since the attack and his insistence, she just hadn't seemed to care much.

"Are you okay?" Zeke's worry hadn't been a product of the military, but of the family he'd created within Stryker

Security Force. To him, family was everything, even if he'd had to create it himself.

"Yeah." Lena sighed and rubbed her sore lower back. "Thankfully, June's Supersuit worked perfectly."

"You were shot?" The words echoed in surround sound as both Zeke and Marshall said them, startling her gaze to Marshall emerging from the bathroom.

His wet hair stuck up in all directions like he'd run the towel over it and hadn't bothered with straightening it. She put her index finger over her lips to quiet him. She couldn't have two conversations at one time.

"Yeah, I may have left a mess in a park in Coeur d'Alene, Idaho." She tried not to watch Marshall as he stepped over Bjørn, already conked out on the floor, but fatigue gnawed at her brain. She'd chalk it up to keeping tabs on everyone. "I took out two of the attackers before we escaped."

"What are your plans now?" Zeke's confidence in her loosened the nerves that had tangled in her stomach while she had sucked up the courage to call.

"Bjørn was picking up a helicopter in Spokane." Lena sighed, doubt at what they were doing creeping back in. "We've decided to take them to my parents' place in Alaska. I worried with Mr. Rand's and June's companies collaborating, the people after him would think Stryker was hiding him. From my parents' place, I'm taking them to the mountains. If my cover held, there shouldn't be any way for Mr. Rand's enemies to make the connection."

She closed her eyes, rubbing her fingers across her lids to ease the dryness. She prayed she was right and that they could find a place to lie low and figure out what was going on. Ever since they'd left Virginia, she hadn't felt like she could breathe fully.

"Smart. I'll get Rafe to reinforce your info and see if anyone has been poking around." Zeke sighed.

A soft touch on her knee snapped her hand down. Marshall rose his eyebrow in question and mouthed, "Are you okay?" Her heart raced faster and faster, like the ice breaking up on the Tanana River in the spring. The more water exposed, the quicker the ice rushed downstream, the big chunks tumbling over each other for the race to the sea. She forced a smile, then scooted farther onto the bed, ignoring the way Marshall's face fell as he settled on the opposite bed beside a sleeping Carter.

"There's more, Zeke." Lena breathed out a sharp breath. "I think the people after the Rands are the same people that attacked June and kidnapped Kiki, Eva, and Derrick."

"What?" Marshall stood fast and sat on the edge of her bed, and she pulled her knees up to her chest to keep from touching him again.

His face filled with intense focus, willing her to tell him what was going on. She held up her hand to halt any questions. She had to fill Zeke in first, then she could get Marshall up to speed. He mouthed, "Speaker." So, with a huff, she clicked the call to speakerphone.

"Why do you think that?" Tapping came through the phone. Zeke's habit of tapping his fingers when he was thinking helped her relax a little more. She wasn't in this by herself. Her team would do anything to help her keep Carter and Marshall safe.

"Well, Marshall was given a note that threatened they'd kill Carter like they killed his wife." She stared at Marshall.

"I thought his wife died in a car accident."

"Apparently not." Sorrow filled Lena for Carter, who would never know his mother and for Marshall, who lost his wife. "Her death was connected to the border bill. The one bill that ..."

She paused, not wanting to speak about Ethan and how Marshall's vote sealed his death. Ever since she'd started working for him, she'd wanted him to know, longed to march into his office and tell him the vivid details of Ethan's death so they could haunt him too. But now, she wasn't so sure. Her righteous anger didn't burn so hot at the moment. She stared at her knees, sick with how easily she'd given up on finding justice for Ethan. Had she really loved him? Not working for the general on his team, and now, not wanting Marshall to know what he did made her think she hadn't really loved Ethan. Not like she should have.

"I know the one, Lena." Anger and grief tinged Zeke's voice. "So, since the same organization has been involved in all those instances, it makes sense it's involved now."

"Yeah." Grief thickened her voice, so she cleared her throat, determined to move this conversation forward. She needed sleep, though she doubted she'd find any tonight. "Have you gotten any updates from Paxton?"

"No, just that every time they think they're close, they find something new that digs them a little deeper." Zeke's statement made her question not going to work for Paxton even more.

"They need more help." She knew it, but was she strong enough to leave what she'd found at Stryker?

"Not from you." Zeke was always good at reading minds.

She pressed the icon to turn the speaker off and put the phone to her ear.

"Why not?" Her hackles rose. Didn't he think she could do it?

"Because I need you on our team, Rebel. You're family."

Zeke's voice dropped. "Besides, you're much too emotional about it, and emotions have no place in war."

"Or I'm exactly what his team needs." Besides, she could control her emotions. No one knew just how much pain and anger she kept locked within.

Marshall shifted, drawing her gaze to him. He stared at her, his eyes skimming over her face like he was trying to figure her out. She turned her head, shuttered her expression, and looked across the room toward the closed blinds. He could search all he wanted, but all he'd find was the shield she wore to protect herself.

"We used the fake passports Rafe made for the Rands to get into Canada. Have him double-check that those are still good." She wanted off this call.

"I'll send someone up to help." Zeke's words sent panic rising up her throat.

"No," she practically shouted, and Carter shifted where he slept on the opposite bed. She lowered her voice. "I don't want to risk that they're watching Stryker, and we lead them right to us."

She also didn't want to risk any more of her team getting hurt by these guys. Zeke would flip a brick if he knew, but she was already putting her family at risk. She didn't want to take any more chances than she had to. Once they made it to the mountains, everyone would be secure, so anyone Zeke sent up would be bored out of their minds.

"Lena."

"Zeke, we'll only be at my parents' long enough to get supplies, then we're heading to the mountains." Lena huffed out a sigh, wishing they could be there now. "The cabin is small, off-grid, and no one knows it's there."

"All right." Doubt was thick in his voice. "But you call if

anything happens, and make sure Bjørn is close to help if needed."

"Copy that." She rubbed her temple at the headache building. "I'll check in when I can."

"Stay alert," Zeke commanded.

"Stay safe," she replied with the rest of the army saying.

The call ended, and her screen went black. Had she made the right decision in not having Zeke send someone up? Doubt clawed up her chest, making it hard to breathe.

"What's this team you're talking about?" Marshall pulled his foot up onto the bed, making himself comfortable when she wanted him to leave. "The one connected to General Paxton?"

"It's classified." Lena set her phone on the nightstand.

"Lena." Marshall's eyes begged her to tell him.

"It's late. I'm exhausted, and we're leaving early." She scooted on the bed and got under the covers.

He stared her down, his face hardening to a stubborn look her brothers often got. Too bad for him that she could be just as stubborn, maybe more. She motioned to the other bed with her head and stretched out on the far side of her bed, away from him.

He didn't move, and Lena closed her eyes and willed herself not to roll over. His harsh breathing behind her voiced his displeasure and possibly shock. Did anyone ever go against his orders? Probably not to his face. A hard huff was followed by the shifting of him getting off the bed.

He deserved to know, especially with what happened to his wife. She didn't think she could explain right now, with her emotions frayed and so close to the surface. Once she got some sleep and some distance from the stress of the day, she'd be able to give a report to him—a clinically detailed report. No grief tainting her words. No fear clouding her thoughts. She could bring him up to speed without giving all the information.

Just who was she protecting, Marshall or herself? A chill froze her core, and she tightened the blanket around her. The light clicked off and plunged the room into darkness, but her mind raced long into the night.

NINE

MARSHALL'S JAW dropped as he stared out the window at the homestead below them while the helicopter made its decent. The Rebel Ranch sat on the east side of a wide valley surrounded by mountains that jutted to the sky. Yet, it wasn't really a ranch at all.

A large log cabin that could easily be featured on any upscale magazine was in the middle of a huge manicured lawn. Birch, aspen, and spruce surrounded the lawn like a reminder that the Alaskan wilderness waited patiently to claim the land as its own. A small creek meandered along one side of the open area, weaving in and out of the trees. Smaller cabins were placed along the creek. Tucked a short walk behind the house, a lake sparkled in the late morning sun, complete with a moose chomping on grass.

Bjørn continued past the main homestead to a landing strip sliced through the trees. Three small planes, quintessentially Alaskan, parked next to a hangar. Exactly what kind of family did Lena come from?

"I thought you said this was a ranch?" He turned and looked between the Rebel siblings.

Lena's mouth turned up on one side as she gazed out her window. That small action shouldn't enthrall him, especially since he was still upset with her. Though she'd had two and a half more days of travel after that first night to clue him in to exactly what was going on, she'd avoided every chance they had to talk. Why couldn't she just tell him? He deserved to know, especially since it involved Amara's death and the border bill that caused her murder.

Bjørn threw his head back and laughed, drawing Marshall back to the present. "My dad started calling it Rebel Ranch back when they first bought it. Said the name had a nice ring to it." Bjørn checked his gauges and window. "The only animals we've ever had are dogs and some annoying chickens my ma babies. The place used to be an old roadhouse along the original highway south toward Anchorage. My parents bought the place, tore down the original building that was falling apart, and built their cabin. Over the years, they've fixed up the original small guest cabins, one that John Wayne stayed in when he was filming *North to Alaska*, and built the other guest cabins. It's gone from a rundown memory to a world-renowned, semi-private retreat. They don't have any guests this week, because of the party, so we'll have the place all to ourselves."

The skids touched down, and Bjørn flipped switches to shut down the engine. Marshall unbuckled and turned to get Carter. Lena already had him out and scrambling to get for the door. Marshall pushed down his frustration. Even when he tried to be a better dad to Carter, he was too slow in jumping to action. Would he ever be able to be the father Carter needed? He shook the question off and grabbed gear as he exited. It didn't help that Lena was great at taking care of his son. What a stupid thing to think. Marshall should be glad that she knew what she was doing, not jealous.

A large, white wolf barreled out of the trees with a vicious bark that rose all the hairs on Marshall's body. He rushed to Carter, who had frozen at the sight of the beast, and lifted his small, trembling body into his arms. Could they get back into the helicopter before the animal attacked?

"Snowflake, no. Calm down." Lena commanded the dog with laughter in her voice.

Marshall turned back to the wolf that wasn't a wolf, his fear transforming to shock as the giant crouched low to the ground, its entire body shaking as its tail wagged. "Snowflake?"

"Embarrassing, isn't it?" Bjørn walked behind him and clapped Marshall on the shoulder as he strapped down the skids. "Our youngest sister named him."

"What exactly is he?" Marshall tightened his hold on Carter as the dog cocked his head to the side like he was deciding if they would taste good.

"He's a Great Pyrenees." Lena rubbed Snowflake's over-sized, hairy head. "My parents keep him around to protect the place from predators. Come on over here, and I'll introduce you."

A hint of a dare edged her voice. Great. Another reason for Lena Rebel to think less of him. At least he'd grabbed up Carter in his puppy terror. He pushed his shoulders back and strode to where she knelt.

"Come on, Carter. Let's go meet Snowflake." Marshall bent next to Lena and reached his hand out to let Snowflake sniff.

Carter trembled in Marshall's arms and buried his face into Marshall's neck. His tiny arms squeezed so tight, Marshall's head might pop off. He sat crisscross in the rough grass and rubbed his son's back.

"Hey, buddy. It's okay." Marshall tried to peel Carter off of him, only causing his little bands of steel to squeeze harder. "Carter, Snowflake here is a friendly dog. He helps keep people safe, and he's really nice. Don't you want to meet him?"

Carter shook his head, his nose rubbing against Marshall's neck. Marshall peeked at Lena, but she just shrugged and continued petting the dog. A lot of help she was. He rubbed his fingers through Snowflake's soft fur by his ear.

"Wow, Carter, you should feel how soft Snowflake's fur is." He hoped he pulled off excitement while keeping his tone calm.

The dog licked Marshall's hand and nudged it when he stopped petting. Marshall chuckled, scratching behind the big ear. As the dog groaned in contentment and thundered his massive tail against the dirt, Carter peeked up at Marshall's face.

"Noflake nice, Daddy?" Interest flashed through the worry on Carter's face.

Marshall smiled down at Carter as he patted him on the back. "Yeah, squirt. Snowflake is nice."

Carter turned to the dog, though he still pushed up against Marshall's body. Marshall wrapped one arm around Carter's stomach to help him feel protected and grabbed his son's hand with his other. The importance of this moment crashed over Marshall. He was helping his son overcome a fear, maybe for the first time ever. Why had he kept himself so busy and missed out on so much?

"If you hold your hand up like this, Snowflake will sniff you and see if he wants to be your friend." Marshall held Carter's hand toward the dog's nose.

When Snowflake stretched out his snout, Carter pulled his hand back and shook his head. "Me scared."

Marshall hugged Carter tightly. "I know you're scared, buddy. Snowflake is a big dog." Marshall smiled as Snowflake laid his body on the ground, whined, and inched himself closer. "I think Snowflake really wants to be your friend. He's sad you're scared of him."

Lena's hand stilled where it had been languidly petting the dog's side. Had he said something wrong again? She rubbed her lip with her other fingers as she stared at Marshall. She offered him a small smile that quickly faded, and looked down at Snowflake, who whined pathetically. Did the smile mean he was doing good?

"Me don't want Noflake sad." Carter's tiny hand shook as he reached it toward the dog.

Snowflake stilled except the minuscule tap of his tail, like he knew he scared Carter. Carter held his hand in front of the dog's nose, glancing up at Marshall for reassurance. Marshall nodded and smiled.

"Perfect. Just let him sniff you," Marshall whispered.

Snowflake sniffed against the back of Carter's hand, and Carter giggled. "Tickles."

"Why don't you pet his fur?" Lena touched Carter's fingers, then touched the side of the dog's face. "He's really soft."

There was something different about Lena's tone. Marshall searched her face for clues of what she was thinking. As he stared, a soft pink touched her cheekbones. Was Lena Rebel blushing? He shook his head and focused back on Carter, who was running his fingers through the white fur. It must just be the way the sun was shining on her face. There was no way that Lena Rebel, the woman who barely tolerated his presence, would blush under his perusal. He shouldn't be perusing her in the first place.

Carter crawled off of Marshall's lap and hugged Snowflake just as an older couple emerged from a trail through the woods. The man resembled Bjørn, with his tall, lean, muscled frame and dark, blond hair, while the woman walking hand in hand with him was petite, probably barely over five feet, and obviously of native descent. So, this was where Lena's exotic looks came from.

"Lena?" Her mother's hand covered her mouth before she took off running toward Lena.

Lena's smile radiated pure joy as she pushed off the ground and rushed to meet her mom. From the moment he'd met Lena, he'd found her attractive. When she showed gentle and loving care to Carter, he had a hard time not staring. With her guard completely down and happiness shining from her, she was stunning.

What had made her so guarded and terse? Did he really want to know, since it seemed to have something to do with him? Maybe now that they were done running, he could make her tell him about this elusive organization and what it had to do with him. If he approached it right, she might confess why she barely tolerated him. Granted, she'd eased up on him since the attack, but he wanted more. The desire to see her smile brightly at him had taken root, and no matter how often or forcefully he argued with himself, he couldn't rip the feeling loose.

TEN

"I DIDN'T KNOW you were coming." Lena's ma squeezed her tightly, her strong hug filling Lena's heart with a love she'd desperately needed.

She'd waited far too long to come home, letting her grief and fear override her need for family. She wanted to punch herself in the face, knock some sense in. In staying away, she'd not only hurt herself, but from the tears sparkling in her ma's eyes, her distance had broken her mother's heart as well.

"Move out of the way, Ma, and let me have my turn." Her father gently pushed Ma out of the way and engulfed Lena into his powerful arms. "What's brought you up here, pumpkin?"

The question pinched with the implication something had forced her to come. The Rebel family was close. Growing up the way they had created a deeply attached family that took devotion to a level she'd rarely seen in other families.

That was probably why she'd glued herself to the Stryker team instead of coming home. They mirrored the

Rebel mold of tenacious devotion to each other, and she'd let that family step in when she couldn't face the emptiness Ethan's death had left in the vast Alaskan wilderness. But brotherly affection and bonding with the girls couldn't replace the hug of her ma or the look of respect and adoration her dad gave as he took her in. While she had buried her dreams of an Alaskan future with Ethan, she didn't need to isolate herself from those who loved her.

"Dad, we ran into a bit of trouble in the lower forty-eight and needed a place to hide out." Lena pulled back and glanced between her parents. "I'm really sorry. We're only staying the night, then I'm taking them to the cabin."

"Nonsense, honey. You all can stay right here." Dad draped his arm over her shoulder and led her back to the Rands.

"No, Dad, we can't." The fear of the organization piecing things together and finding her family bunched her muscles with tension. It was a mistake to have come here. If something happened to her parents, she'd never forgive herself. "It's too dangerous for you. It'll be safer for everyone if we disappear into the wilderness."

"We can take care of any trouble that comes this way." His offended scoff made her lips twitch.

She didn't doubt her Alaskan born and raised parents could handle any problem they faced. They had an arsenal that rivaled even the Stryker's artillery, but she'd witnessed the destruction and deprecation the people they were up against could inflict. She couldn't risk it.

"I know, Dad." She patted his hand on her shoulder as they walked to meet Marshall and Carter. "My team and I have a plan." Not completely a lie. "I need to get this family to my cabin."

"Well, if you're sure." His voice trailed off, like he

wanted her to change her mind.

She wasn't sure, but it was the only plan she had at the moment. Marshall scrambled to his feet as they approached. His eyes bounced from her parents to her, his gaze holding hers and making her chest tight. There was something different in his expression, something she hadn't seen before. The intensity of it had her chest and neck warming, and she ducked her head in embarrassment.

Lena Rebel didn't do embarrassed ... or blushing innocence, for that matter.

All that started and stopped with Ethan Stryker. She peeked up to find Marshall's lips tweaking up in a grin. At least, she thought it had ended. She really shouldn't have let her guard down.

Her dad's eyebrow rose as he looked between Lena and Marshall, and his smile broadened when he reached out his hand to Marshall. "Welcome to our home. I'm Arne Rebel, and this is my wife, Katie."

Lena would have to squash whatever thoughts ran through her dad's head and made that eyebrow lift. Lena stepped from under Dad's arm and strode to the helicopter. She didn't want her parents getting any ideas.

"I'm so glad you all made it for the party." Her ma gushed, bending down to talk to Carter. "Looks like you've found a friend."

"Noflake nice. He's my friend." Carter gave Snowflake a hug.

Lena wished she could get over her fears as fast as Carter. She'd gotten good at hiding them, and she'd learned early in her childhood that even when you were afraid, you could still act. Growing up in the Alaskan wilderness didn't leave room for getting frozen in fear. How would life look if her fear of losing those closest to her didn't cause her to push everyone away?

Wow, Lena, really? There were more important things to worry about. Like not dying, for one. She dropped a duffle of clothes and supplies they'd picked up in Canada at Marshall's feet and hiked her backpack farther up her shoulder.

"Party? What party?" Poor Marshall.

He'd been so confused over the last few days. Lena really needed to do better at clueing him in. Not wanting to talk about the organization and his, albeit unknown, involvement with them, she'd mastered the distract and evade method while traveling. It should thrill her to finally expose his actions for what they'd done. She'd been dreaming of how she'd do that since she'd first started researching that stupid bill two years before. Now, though, her need for justice had cooled, hardening to a boulder of indecision in her gut.

"Oh, nothing big, really. Just family coming over to celebrate our anniversary." Leave it to Ma to downplay what would probably be an afternoon of chaos.

"You don't mind us crashing it?" Marshall glared at Lena before picking up the duffle and slinging it over his shoulders.

"Are you kidding?" Dad draped his arm over Lena's shoulders and rocked her back and forth like a child. "You brought our long-lost Lena back. You're welcome to stay as long as you want. Move in, even. We've got plenty of room."

Lena's face burned hot as she elbowed him in the side. "Dad."

"Carter, would you like to help me make the snacks?" Ma stood and held out her hand.

"Noflake come too?" Carter squeezed Snowflake's head like he worried they would leave the dog behind.

Ma's laugh flitted through the air like a chickadee's song, lifting Lena's spirit. "Of course, Snowflake can come."

"How long have you been married?" Marshall asked as he helped Carter get untangled from the dog.

Dad threaded his fingers through Ma's and lifted them to his lips for a soft kiss. "Not long enough."

The words slammed into Lena, knocking the breath from her. She'd wanted a life filled with love like her parents had. Ethan had been her forever. One corrupted mission and a bullet to the chest later, her happily ever after had bled from her life.

"Not long enough." Marshall's quiet echo pulled her from the shock of grief.

He flinched, his Adam's apple bobbing like he'd swallowed something whole. How could she forget that his love had been ripped away as well? The same people that had taken Ethan had blown apart Marshall's happy family. Her pulse roared in her ears, drowning everything out and slowing the world around her.

Maybe Marshall wasn't an enemy after all.

Devastation had crashed over his life just like it had hers. Worse when Carter was added to the equation. Marshall's hand rubbed his wrist as he watched Lena's parents head toward the house with Carter. She followed his gaze in time to see her dad pull her mom close and kiss the side of her head.

She trudged after her parents, her head spinning with questions. Could she forgive Marshall for his role in Ethan's death? Could she forgive herself if she did? She wasn't sure, and the warring in her mind weighed her body down and made her sluggish. Somehow, she had to push the questions aside and focus. She couldn't keep Marshall and Carter safe if she allowed her doubts and troubles to distract her.

ELEVEN

MARSHALL STOOD ON THE PORCH, taking in the scene before him. Chaos reigned as the Rebel family played touch football on the lawn. It had struck him as odd seeing the expanse of green that would rival any country-club landscaping back in Kentucky. How was it possible to create such perfection in the wilds of Alaska?

But as he'd met each Rebel sibling, and chatted with Arne and Katie, he had realized that if the Rebels set out to tame the wilderness, they'd succeeded. It wouldn't surprise Marshall if a pet moose came trotting on to the field. What was it about this family that had produced such successful and adventure-driven people? They seemed to thrive on danger, each picking paths that most never considered.

Between the seven siblings there was a retired pararescueman with the Air Force, who was now training for the nation's most difficult dogsled race, the Yukon Quest. Becoming a PJ was one of the harshest programs the military offered. There was a bush pilot and hunting guide, a wildfire fighter, a fishing boat captain, and a Denali summit guide. That didn't include Lena and Bjørn, who were both decorated, retired soldiers. All that greatness stuffed in one family left Marshall with a sense of lacking.

Marshall flinched as Lena barreled into her PJ brother, Gunnar, knocking the man to the ground with an audible grunt. Marshall couldn't imagine what a tackle game of football would look like. He shook his head and checked on Carter. He happily played in the sandbox on the side of the yard with Snowflake keeping guard.

His son had slid into the family like he'd always belonged, soaking in the attention of each adult like he was a parched cactus during a drought. Marshall, on the other hand, had never felt as much of an outsider as he did at that moment. He'd never questioned his ability to protect and provide like he did on this ranch full of heroes.

"Don't let them intimidate you, son." Arne stepped up beside Marshall on the deck, leaned his forearms against the railing, and cradled his steaming mug of coffee in his hands. "They may be rowdy, but they're all a good bunch."

Marshall forced a laugh as Sunny, the Denali guide who had just finished leading her last climb up the treacherous mountain for the season, clotheslined Magnus, the wildfire fighter, whose tall form and muscular build was the epitome of a chainsaw-wielding sawyer. "If I go out there, I'm dead."

"Nah. They only play rough with each other." Arne sipped from his coffee. "Here in the Interior, you either grow up tough or you don't grow up at all." He chuckled as the bush pilot brother, Teekhan, dove and grabbed Sunny around the ankles, sending her face-first into the grass. "As they got older, the play just got rougher, like they had to make up for the months, sometimes years, they're not able to be around each other."

"I only have one younger sister who wanted nothing to do with me growing up." Marshall huffed a laugh with the memory. "I wouldn't play dolls with her. But this." He motioned to the grown adults tumbling over each other like children. "This is something I can honestly say I've never experienced ... or known I wanted until today."

The last part was just a whisper, but Arne turned to face Marshall with a questioning look on his face. "Just what brings you running here, son?"

"Some people want me to change course in my business and political influence. It's an organization that I know little about but seems to be a bigger part of my life than I ever realized." Marshall took a deep breath and turned so his back leaned against the railing. "They threatened Carter, then showed up in Idaho, where we had gone to lie low so I could figure things out. Apparently, my head of security is also on their payroll."

Arne whistled low and motioned to the lounge chairs up against the house. He eased back and relaxed into the seat, but Marshall sat on the edge of his. His unease and inability to keep Carter safe kept him from relaxing. Maybe it would be better if he left Carter here? Surely it would be easier for Lena to keep Carter safe if she didn't have to worry about his father too. Marshall knew he couldn't stay forever. He had responsibilities that had to be considered, but the thought of leaving Carter chilled him to the bone.

"What happened in Idaho, and how'd you meet up with Bjørn?" Arne took another long drink of his coffee.

"With the help of my security guy, Tony, two other men got the drop on us." A shiver ran down Marshall's spine at the memory, and he slumped back against the seat to hide his discomfort. "Thankfully, the other two men on my detail weren't traitors, and when Lena jabbed Tony in the throat, they gave us enough time to get away. We don't even know if my men are alive or dead or what." He swallowed down the guilt of leaving his men. His eyes followed Lena, taunting Bjørn with the football. "Lena was incredible." Marshall's voice held too much awe, so he cleared his throat to hide his building attraction. "She had escape plans all laid out in her head and got us out of there within seconds."

He clenched his fists as he remembered the two shots she took to the back. Thank God for June Rivas's Supersuit, otherwise Lena would be dead, and Marshall and Carter would be in the hands of the enemy. He'd leave that part of the adventure out. He doubted Arne would want to hear that Marshall had almost gotten his daughter killed.

"She's always had contingency plans, in camping and hunting, in paths for her future. Always prepared, that's my Lena." Arne sighed a deep sound that came from his toes, and he set his coffee on the side table. "But after Ethan's death, her paranoia and need to always be on guard have gone too far."

"Ethan?"

"Ethan Stryker, her fiancé." Arne shook his head in sadness. "Their team was sabotaged on a mission two years ago, and Ethan got shot in the chest. Lena and Ethan's wedding was supposed to be the next week."

Marshall's vision tunneled as pieces clicked into place. Stryker Security Force was named for a man killed in action. Lena's conversation with Zeke popped into Marshall's head. Somehow, the organization after him was involved with the death of her fiancé.

"Apparently a bill passed legislation that stripped the team of tech they used on missions. One minute the tech was there. The next it was unavailable." Arne *tsked*. "Lena's been obsessed with that bill, with figuring out how it passed in the first place. Says that Ethan and other soldiers that were killed because of that bill need justice."

"It's my fault. I'm the one who voted that bill in." Marshall closed his eyes as he tried to take a deep breath but failed. "That's why she hates me."

He didn't deserve her protection. Didn't deserve her putting her life on the line for him. Would that one mistake haunt him forever? He thought of Lena's aloofness that hid her anger and pain at losing the man she loved. Thought of all the men and women lost because he hadn't been stronger in his convictions. He earned never finding peace the day he voted yes to a law that put the nation's frontline at risk.

"How's that?" Arne touched Marshall's elbow.

Marshall opened his eyes and stared at the jutting mountains on the edge of the property. He couldn't bear to see the disappointment that Arne would feel when Marshall revealed his deceit. When the truth was laid out, Marshall would retreat to the room Katie had given him and Carter so this family that had sacrificed so much wouldn't have to look at him.

"I was the vote that put that bill into law." Marshall spoke low, remembering the conflict and grief that had raged within him as he put his yes down. "I knew there was more buried in the bill that we didn't understand. The thing was a tome and being pushed through quickly. There wasn't time to read it, let alone understand it."

"Why'd you vote to pass it then?"

"My wife, she begged me to support it. Said a law that beefed up the borders couldn't be bad." He rubbed his hand down his face as shame heated his skin. "When she died in a car crash the day before we voted, I let my grief overrule my logic and checked yes in honor of Amara." He snorted a humorless laugh. "Come to find out, she never really wanted it to pass. She was being threatened, told if she didn't convince me to back the bill, then something bad would happen to our family." He touched the pocket where her journal entry hid. "If I would've been paying more attention to her, I would've known something was wrong. I could've protected her. Wouldn't have betrayed Lena's fiancé and the other soldiers. It's my fault that bill passed."

"Son." Arne leaned over and placed his hand on Marshall's shoulder, causing him to flinch. "How many other members of Congress voted for that bill?"

"That's not the point." Marshall scooted to the edge of his seat and shook his head. "I promised my constituents that I would lead in the push toward healing our country, but I betrayed them and allowed others to use me to hurt the soldiers I swore to support." He turned to Arne, his eyes burning with angry tears. "Did you know that was my running platform? I promised to strengthen our nation and always stand behind our troops. Always. The people surrounding Fort Knox would expect nothing less from their representative. And I let them down." He waved his hand to the Rebels still playing in the yard. "I let them all down."

"We all make mistakes, and there were two hundred and seventeen other members of Congress who share in that blame with you." Arne shifted to the edge of his seat and leaned his forearms on his knees. "Yet you're the only one I've seen making amends. What have you done to correct that mistake since you voted?"

"It doesn't matter." Marshall hung his head. "It can never make up for all those I hurt. Never make up for Lena losing Ethan. For Amara being murdered."

"That's where you're wrong." Arne's sharp jab to Marshall's bicep hurt. "If I remember right, for the rest of your term in Congress, you did everything you could to shift the current political landscape while transforming your entire billion-dollar company back in Kentucky to assist in the production of tools for the military."

"How do you know all that?"

"When Lena became obsessed with it, I started researching." Arne's lips twisted up in a slight grin beneath his dark blond beard. "When she called to tell us she would be working for you, I wondered how she'd handle it."

"She hates me. After what I did, I don't blame her." He stared at Lena, who had stopped playing football to sit with Carter.

He swallowed the longing that had grown toward her, stuffing it deep down in the never-gonna-happen part of his brain, and slammed the door closed. If he couldn't see past his own disgust and regrets, what made him think she ever would? Being up here was a mistake. He would never find answers and couldn't continue his fight against this evil if he stayed hidden. He'd get them settled wherever it was Lena wanted them to hide out, then talk Bjørn into getting him to an airport. Knowing Carter was safe and putting some distance between his growing desire for Lena would let him focus on his goal. He couldn't support the military and reduce corruption in the legislature if he was hiding in the Alaskan wilderness.

"Lena doesn't hate you, not really," Arne said.

Marshall snorted and shook his head, though Arne's words raised a pathetic sense of hope within him.

"She may have at first, but Lena isn't dumb. If I found out all that about you, she would have too." Arne clapped Marshall's shoulder. "I'm praying hard for her. She needs to forgive, to let God heal her, but the longer and tighter she holds on to that anger, she'll never find peace."

Peace. Marshall's nose stung as he fought to control his emotions. What would it feel like to have a peaceful heart

again, to have joy overpower the regret and pain? Was there
any possibility he and Lena could find it together?

"Maybe ... maybe you could pray for me too?" He
breathed past the tightness in his chest and looked at Arne.

Arne squeezed his shoulder. "I already am, son. I
already am."

Marshall bit the inside of his cheek and turned back to
the yard. Carter threw himself at Lena. The smiles
stretched across both their faces had salmons flipping in
Marshall's stomach. He was ready to put his grief behind
him and find a happy life with Carter. Maybe, just maybe,
he could convince Lena to want the same.

TWELVE

LENA SAT on the outdoor loveseat she'd built with her dad in middle school and stared across the calm lake. Swallows danced and flipped through the air as they chased mosquitos. The flap of wings echoed loud in the peaceful night, and Lena held her breath as an eagle lifted from a tree and dove to the lake. Gosh, she'd missed this place.

The midnight sun skimmed low on the northern horizon, stretching the shadows of the black spruce into long, twisted forms of the originals. She'd always said the short trees looked like a bunch of old men with long shaggy hair and hunched and twisted bodies. Now, as the sun filtered through the sparse limbs, she couldn't help but think she'd come to resemble them.

Being home with her family showed her that.

When had she become so twisted and haggard of spirit? She'd always pictured herself like the black spruce on the other side of the property. They grew in rich soil that could support the roots and allowed the trees to grow tall and straight ... proud. As a child, she'd lain beneath them, staring up into the crisscrossing branches, vowing she'd be strong like the trees she loved.

Somewhere along the line, she'd lost a part of herself. She'd planted herself square in the boggy muskegs life had thrown at her. There was no doubt she was strong and resilient, just like the twisted spruce that grew above the harsh Alaskan permafrost. But inside, she felt dark, like she barely held on. As if someone could come along and, with one small push, knock her over, roots and all. Was it possible for her to get back into good soil, to find a way out of the frigid existence she now found herself in?

She closed her eyes and breathed in the crisp, fresh Alaskan air so different from the Kentucky humidity she'd spent the last few months in. Could she let go of the burning need to avenge Ethan's senseless death? His face flashed before her closed lids, the cocky smile that had said he could take on anything, even a stubborn, no-nonsense girl from the bush. She snapped her eyes open, her breath bottling up in her chest. No. She couldn't dishonor Ethan's memory by not doing everything she could. She'd already betrayed him with her growing attraction to Marshall.

"Can I join you?" Her mother's soft question startled Lena and proved just how out of sync with her surroundings she was.

On the other hand, her ma had always walked on silent feet. She probably would have startled Lena anyway. Lena scooted to one side of the bench and shrugged.

"Thought you'd be in bed by now." Lena peeked up at her ma. The yoga pants and sweatshirt didn't diminish her regal posture.

Lena and her sisters had often speculated that their ma descended from some tribal royalty, a princess warrior from their Athabaskan past. The Rebel sisters varied in their appearances. Lena and Sunny took after their mom, while Astryd was more fair like their Norwegian father. Yet, they all had wanted to be like Ma. They'd marveled at their mother's strength and how she was smarter, braver, and more beautiful than most people they knew. The years since Lena's childhood hadn't changed her mother much, but for maybe a few more laugh lines around her eyes.

Ma sat and turned to Lena, the merriment that had so often filled their home replaced by lines of worry. "Why are you out here after midnight staring off across the lake?"

Lena shrugged. "Just couldn't sleep is all."

"No, it's more than that." Her ma pushed Lena's hair behind her shoulder.

Lena took a deep breath, stalling while she gathered her thoughts. But the more she tried to reign them in, the more they scattered and rolled about like a dumped bucket of cranberries. She huffed in frustration.

"I'm just confused, I guess." Maybe she could tell her mom part of her troubles, then scurry away and hide before Ma ferreted out all of her thoughts. "I had plans to join this special team hunting down the people who are conspiring against the nation, the ones responsible for Ethan's death, but now I'm here, with no clue how long we'll be holed up on the mountain."

Her mom nodded and gazed across the lake. "Why does that bother you? Do you not want to keep Carter and his dad safe?"

"No, it's not that."

"Are you worried about protecting them?" Ma's calm question rattled Lena.

"No."

"Are they horrible people?"

"Ma, please, you've met them." Lena rolled her eyes.

"Then why are you wanting to go somewhere else when you are needed here?"

"Because ..." Lena grasped for a plausible reason before blurting out what was on her heart. "Because how can I find vengeance for Ethan's death when I'm not out there searching for those who took him from me? How can I work for the man whose vote put the bullet in Ethan's chest? How can I—"

She stopped herself before she said any more. She couldn't say what she'd been thinking. She could never take it back once it was out.

"How can you betray Ethan by being attracted to Marshall?" Her mom's soft question snapped Lena's head back like a jab to the nose.

A lump formed in her throat as she shook her head in denial.

"Please, Lena. That man is hotter than a sled dog in July."

Lena snorted, choking as she inhaled. "Ma!"

They laughed, the sound floating across the smooth water to flit about with the swallows. Lena crossed her ankles and clenched her fingers around the edge of the seat. It didn't matter how hot Marshall was. Guilt weighed heavily on her and curved her shoulders inward. How could she possibly find anything about him attractive when he hadn't stood behind the military like he'd promised?

Lena stared at the grass in front of her feet. She had to be the most disloyal person she knew. She needed to stuff down these traitorous feelings for Marshall, didn't she? She couldn't be attracted to the enemy, the man who betrayed his country and the men and women protecting it. What kind of soldier was she if she did? What kind of fiancée? Her nose tingled and eyes burned with emotions she refused to let fall.

"Did you know I was engaged before your father?" Ma pulled her knees up to her chest and wrapped her arms around her legs.

Lena turned her head to her ma, searching for any mention of a fiancé in her memories. "I thought you and Dad had been high school sweethearts?"

A pained expression crossed her ma's face. "No. We weren't."

"But Dad always says he loved you since you were kids." Her skin tingled with the discomfort of the falsehood. Why had her parents lied all these years?

"He did." Ma sighed. "I loved him, too, just not in the way he loved me. He was my best friend. We did everything together growing up. Living up in Chicken, year-round gold mining didn't leave us with a lot of options for friends. Not that it would've mattered. Your father and I were stuck like glue from the moment his family moved up there."

Lena tucked her foot under her knee and twisted on the seat so she could really look at her ma. If she was going to find out her idea of a perfect relationship was about to fall apart, she wanted to face the news head on. Did she want to know the truth? Maybe she should stop her ma from telling her story.

"A new family showed up in Chicken for the summer when I was a freshman in high school. Their son, James, was your dad's age and fit right in with us, traipsed around the wilderness until he left with his family for their winter home." A small smile lifted one side of Ma's mouth. "The next summer when he returned, something had shifted between us. James and I started dating." She shook her head. "I could tell it upset your father, but, at the time, I didn't understand why, and he never told me. I just chalked it up to the hormones of a seventeen-year-old boy." Her voice grew quiet. "But really, I just didn't want to see how I had hurt Arne."

Ma paused and stared across the lake. The silence stretched between them, and Lena wondered if she'd hear the rest of the story. She knew life growing up in the small gold-mining community had been a different lifestyle than she understood. The summer exploding the population to over a hundred, with people coming in to mine the Forty Mile district, then winter dwindling the community to a handful of resilient families who loved being isolated from the world. Few kids lived up there year-round. From Dad's childhood tales, all he had was Ma, and Lena couldn't imagine his heartache when her ma started dating someone other than him, especially someone who was a part-timer.

"Anyway, James and I got engaged the next summer." Ma pulled the cuffs of her sweatshirt over her hands.

"But you were only sixteen!" Lena's mouth gaped open.

"That didn't matter. We were in love, and it was a different time." Ma waved it away like it was no big deal. "He and Arne were going off to college in the fall, and James had a plan. He'd do his first year at college, then we'd get married the next summer. I'd be done with high school by then, since I was doubling up, so we could go to college together."

"What happened?"

"Your dad and James went bear hunting one evening." Her voice cracked, and she cleared her throat. "They were walking into the bait stand when a grizzly charged out of the brush. Your father stumbled and tripped, and, well, he accidentally shot James."

Lena gasped and covered her mouth. Her poor father. How horrible that must have been. His intense training on gun safety made sense now.

"I hated your dad, was convinced he did it out of jealousy." Ma winced and closed her eyes. "I was so angry and hurt. The sadness and grief just consumed me until all I saw was hate. I never thought about what Arne was going through, the guilt he carried. All I thought about was my own pain."

"Why didn't you ever tell us?"

"It's not something your dad talks about." Ma shrugged. "As a soldier, you know how that is, Lena. There are some hurts where getting past them means leaving them in the past."

Hadn't Lena seen that over and over again with her military friends? They got help or talked to someone so they could leave the pain behind. Why hadn't she done that with her own hurt? She had so many regrets pushed down deep, so many soldiers she hadn't been able to save, most of all Ethan. It surprised her they all didn't explode within her. How could her ma have ever forgiven her dad?

"But you married Dad." She recoiled at the condemnation in her voice.

"It took me a long time and God forcing us together for me to realize my inability to forgive him not only punished Arne for something he already held more guilt than he should, but had also made me into a bitter, unpleasant person." Her ma's words cut a little too close to Lena's heart. "We're a lot the same, Lena. We have a tendency to hold on to things we should let go of."

"I can't let Ethan go." Her chest ached, and she pressed

a hand over her heart to hold it in. "Besides, what happened with Dad was an accident. Marshall made a conscious decision to vote that horrid bill in."

"From what your Dad told me after talking with the man, he's been doing everything he can to make up for that mistake." Ma's voice was steeped with lenience that a mother of seven rambunctious kids developed over constant tests to her patience. "Have you ever even talked to him about it, or have you just been caught up in your own misery?"

"He's my boss." Lena stood abruptly and stalked to the edge of the lake. "I don't need to know his reasons. All I need to do is focus on the job."

"You've never had a problem with focus, Lena. That's for sure."

The creak of the wooden bench caused Lena to tense. She didn't want to think about this anymore. She couldn't handle the emotions over Marshall and her grief and guilt simmering below the surface, let alone the mix her ma's story had thrown in. If she didn't tighten the lid on herself, she worried it'd all boil over. How could she do her job and keep Carter safe if that happened?

Her ma's hand gently squeezed her shoulder. "I wonder, though, if you're focusing on the wrong things?" She wrapped Lena's shoulders in a one-armed hug. "Don't let your inability to forgive darken your heart, Lena. You won't find all the blessings meant for your future if you do." She kissed the side of Lena's head and let go. "Ethan will always hold the love of your past, but he'd be devastated if you let his memory destroy the love of your future. Maybe you should focus on that for a while."

Ma left as quietly as she came, but Lena's mind hadn't calmed. Could she forgive Marshall, or would that betray

Ethan's memory? She swallowed the sharp pain lodged in her throat and closed her eyes. Did she have the strength to step from the unstable muskeg she'd planted herself in and root herself in soil that would allow her to grow? She wasn't sure, and it scared her that she might not even be brave enough to try.

THIRTEEN

MARSHALL STOOD on the deck of Lena's small, remote cabin, staring across the mountaintops stretching out across the horizon. Could he get any closer to the top of the world? The beauty took his breath away, and being stuck out in the middle of nowhere suddenly didn't seem so bad.

"Daddy, you's has to see this." Carter barreled out of the cabin and snagged Marshall's hand.

His son's enthusiasm stretched his chest with joy. This time with Carter had shown Marshall just how much he wanted things to change when they got back home. He didn't want to be gone all hours of the day, didn't want to be so focused on saving the world that his own world drifted away.

How could he find balance, though? Between the company and DC, time slipped through his hands faster than he could control. The tighter he gripped, the more quickly the moments evaporated. Carter smiled back at Marshall as he dragged him into the cabin, and a jolt coursed through his body. He just needed to analyze everything better, formulate an action plan. Mission: Get Life Back couldn't be that hard if he put his focus into it.

He stopped short as he crossed the threshold. The small, unassuming cabin exuded a rustic opulence he wasn't expecting. Floor to ceiling windows allowed the bright summer sun to bathe the open living space in cheery light. A rich, coffee-colored leather loveseat and a recliner sat on a deep cranberry-red area rug and cozied up to a wood stove. On the other side of the room, cast iron skillets hung on the log wall. Cabinets lined the wood and were topped with what looked like hewn logs for a counter. The space was homey yet functional, upscale but unassuming. How it had been built with no access and nothing close amazed him.

"Daddy, look at the bear." Carter pointed to a big grizzly hanging over the windows and front door behind Marshall. "Eena shot dat bear."

Carter's eyes, wide as saucers, looked up at the animal in awe. Marshall was pretty awestruck himself. He scooped up his son and pointed to the grizzly's three-inch claws.

"That's a gigantic bear, for sure." Marshall peered at Carter's profile. "Do you think Lena was scared?"

Carter's head shook. "Nope. Eena's not a'scared of nothing." The confidence in his tiny voice amused Marshall.

The kid was perceptive. Lena Rebel didn't seem to have the word fear in her vocabulary. It intimidated Marshall and invigorated him at the same time.

"You two are going to be in the sheep room." Lena's voice preceded her as she stepped from the back of the cabin. "Why don't you come and put your stuff down, then we can help Bjørn with the rest of the supplies?"

Marshall set Carter down and hiked the bag slung over his shoulder up. Lena's smile as Carter dashed through the living room with a whoop had Marshall's heart thumping against his ribs. Would she smile at him too? He rolled his eyes at himself when she turned away without even a glance. He wasn't some tongue-tied teenager anymore. There was no reason for him to be disappointed in her lack of attention or for his palms to get sweaty at the thought of being alone with her and Carter on the mountain.

When Marshall stepped into the small room, his estimation of the place rose even further. The room held a bunk bed and a single made from logs and decked out with rustic bedding. A snow-white Dall sheep skin hung on one wall, and two large windows sported views of the rocky mountaintops surrounding them. Every area of the cabin brought the Alaskan range inside, creating an intimate embrace with nature.

He could easily see wanting to just stay in bed and look out across the vistas. What was this place used for? Was it a family retreat, a place to escape? Was it a business lodge, and he was costing them revenue from guests? He'd have to ask Lena and make sure this family, who had so graciously taken in a pair of runaways, got compensated for their generosity.

"My room is right across the hall, and there's a bathroom between us." Lena pointed through the door, quickly dropping her hand when it brushed Marshall's arm in the small space. "We have to haul water up, so we'll need to be conservative."

"All right. No pampering in long showers." Marshall tossed his bag onto one of the beds.

Lena's mouth tweaked up like his comment amused her, and the disappointment of earlier flew out the window. She'd been doing that more and more lately, or maybe it was that being stuck with her gave him a chance to see who she really was. Even more encouraging was the fact it didn't hold the derision it would have two weeks before. Arne's words about Lena not hating him came to mind, and Marshall wondered again if her father might be right.

He didn't want to get his hopes up, but the thought emboldened him. He took a step closer. When her eyebrow rose in a what-do-you-think-you're-doing look, he stifled a grin at her spunk.

"Lena, thank you for all of this." He touched her elbow and sparks shot up his fingers at the feel of her soft skin. "I don't know how I can ever thank you for saving us and keeping us safe."

She stared up at him. When she didn't yank her arm from his touch, he inched closer. Her forehead furrowed as she studied his face. Could he be brave and take the risk? When he jumped from the safety of the walls he'd built, would he land intact or splat in a bigger mess than he already was?

The screen door squeaked open, followed by a grunt and a slam. Lena stepped back and bumped into a bench behind her. Her eyebrows pushed even closer together as her gaze darted to Carter and back.

"I'm going to help Bjørn." She swallowed and pushed past Marshall. "Go ahead and stay here with Carter."

Marshall stared at the mountains. His heart beat wildly in his chest like he'd just played a game of one-on-one and come out victorious. He pursed his lips together to keep his smile in check. He was done analyzing if he should or shouldn't give in to his attraction. For the first time in years, he finally saw through his grief to the possibility of finding happiness again. Now, he'd just have to convince Lena that he wasn't the enemy.

FOURTEEN

"LET'S get the rest of the gear," Lena snapped at Bjørn as she stomped through the living room.

Her ears heated to lava levels as she jogged down the stairs and headed toward the helicopter. Darn her mom and the thoughts she had planted in Lena's head. Since the conversation the night before, the minute she let the guard on her mind down, it spun with possibilities.

What if she let her heart forgive?

Would she not feel such crushing darkness trapping her anymore?

"Hey." Bjørn pushed her shoulder as he stepped up beside her. "You had a nice blush going on back there. Mind telling me what that's all about?"

"Mind your own business," she snapped back, cringing at her sharp tone.

"Sheesh, Lena. Ease up." He grabbed her elbow and pulled her to a stop. "I'm joking. You know, that fun bantering we used to live for?"

"I'm not in the mood for your joking right now."

"You're never in the mood." He threw his hands up in exasperation, stomped toward his helicopter, then turned and stomped back. "I understand you needed time to grieve. I know what that mission cost you. It's been tearing me up that I couldn't help you, that I couldn't do anything to help the team get out sooner."

His anger deflated as his shoulders slumped and he looked off down the valley. She didn't want to talk about that mission. She didn't want to see Ethan's blood saturating his sleeve. Didn't want to relive her own life draining from her as reality crashed in. She held her hands up to ward off any more talk.

"Do you know how many nights I lie awake, wondering if I should've found a closer extraction point?" Bjørn ignored her silent pleas to stop, his question sending ice down her spine. "I could've relayed a closer rendezvous when things blew up. The map had shown a clearing closer to the compound I could've landed in. What if getting Ethan to you earlier would have saved him? Maybe then, Jake wouldn't have lost his leg." His voice cracked, and he cleared his throat. "Maybe then, your world wouldn't have crumbled to what you have now."

"That wasn't your fault. You couldn't have known how bad the mission would go." She never thought pushing her family away in her grief would make Bjørn's healing harder.

He sighed and rubbed his hand over his neck. "I'm ready for a new life now. I'm ready to put all the heartache of failed missions behind me." He shook his head and met her gaze. "It's past time for you to leave it behind too."

"I ... I can't." She blinked to clear the sting from her eyes.

"Ethan wouldn't want this life of loneliness and bitter hate for you." He stepped closer and pointed his finger at her heart. "He'd want you to live and find happiness, not wallow in your fear, pushing everyone away. You're being a coward, Lena." He poked her in the shoulder. "Knock it off before you push so many people away that all you're left with are ghosts."

FIFTEEN

MARSHALL JOGGED to keep up with Lena as she led him and Carter on a hike down the mountain. Carter pulled Marshall's hair like reins on a horse from where his son sat on his shoulders. He was glad of the chance to get outside and explore but would probably have sore shoulders the next morning.

When they'd gotten settled, had lunch, and Carter's level of energy hadn't wavered, Lena had suggested going on a bear hunt like in Carter's favorite book. Marshall wondered if her sudden suggestion had just as much to do with her own restlessness as it did Carter's. Since Bjørn left, she'd been antsy, which made him anxious.

"So, Lena, I've been meaning to ask you about the cabin." He stepped up beside her as they pushed through an alpine meadow. Bright pink fireweed filled the area and drenched the hillside in cheery color. "How in the world did y'all build it on the mountaintop? Does your family use it for business, or is it just a personal cabin?"

"Well ... the cabin is mine, actually." Lena's interest in the ground before them became more intense.

"Yours?"

"Yeah. I built it in high school." She shrugged like constructing a cabin in the middle of nowhere in your teens was no big deal. "My plan was to run a hunting-guide operation out of it after I got out of the military. You know, get the big game like sheep and grizzly away from the normal hunting spots."

"You had that all planned out in high school?" He'd had a plan for his future, but while she'd been building a luxury resort, he hadn't done more than get good grades and excel in basketball to put that plan in action.

She shrugged again and shifted the rifle slung across her shoulders like she was uncomfortable. Why would she even go into the military if she'd already had the cabin built? The more mysteries he unearthed of her, the more confused he got.

"Why not just start guiding right after high school?" Marshall eased Carter's fingers loose when their grip got too tight on his hair. "Why even join the army?"

"Hunting can be dangerous, and being way up here, even more so. I knew I'd need medical training in case of emergency, so I figured I'd let the army do that for me and get paid while doing it." She chuckled, and the tension eased from her shoulders a bit. "I really wanted to be a PJ, pararescuer with the Air Force, like my older brother Gunnar was, but I quickly realized my likelihood of getting through the training to be a PJ was pretty much non-existent. I mean, if Gunnar almost failed, there was no way I could pass."

While in the Air Force, Marshall had often wondered what it would be like to be the bigger-than-life heroes of the military world. PJs rescued downed SEALS while Marshall had analyzed data. His military career never seemed as lacking as it did when measured against the Rebel family.

"You became an army medic so you could be prepared if the worst happened hunting." Marshall's forehead scrunched in confusion. "If that was the point of enlisting, why didn't you come here after you got out?"

She sighed, and the tension bunched back in her shoulders. Maybe he should just keep his questions to himself.

"After Ethan died and I left the army, I just couldn't bring myself back here." She scanned the meadow, looking everywhere but at Marshall. "We had planned on coming up here together, to build a couple more cabins and really make a go of it. When he died, I never thought I'd come back again. Had actually been planning on selling it to Tiikâan for his guiding business."

Guilt coated Marshall's throat and made it hard to swallow. First, he'd been responsible for her fiancé's death. Then, his situation had forced her to face the one place she didn't want to be. Hadn't he felt the same every time he'd walked into his and Amara's bedroom back home after her death? It was the reason he'd moved to the room down the hall. If the house hadn't been in her family for generations, he would have sold it within the month of her dying.

"And now my situation has forced you to come here." He adjusted his grip on Carter's legs to keep from reaching out to her. "I'm sorry, Lena. I'm sorry for everything."

She turned her face to him, her mouth tipping up on one side. "It's okay. You didn't know."

Why did her words seem like they held more weight than they should?

"Daddy, ook!" Carter wiggled and pointed down the slope, almost falling off in his excitement.

An orange fox with a white-tipped tail stood in the

center of the meadow, staring at them. When its head cocked to the side like it wondered where they'd come from, Carter squealed again and tried to get down. Lena stepped closer to Marshall and placed her hand on Carter's leg to settle him.

"Carter, if we're real still and quieter than a mouse, the fox might hang out a while." Lena glanced up at Carter, her voice a soft whisper. "Think you can do that?"

"Like when we payed lions and 'nuck up on Mrs. White and 'cared her?" Carter's return whisper was so full of thrill, Marshall wasn't sure what the kid was more excited about, the fox or the memory of freaking the cook out.

Marshall turned his face to Lena and lifted his eyebrow in question.

"What?" Her face held the expression of false innocence. "The nannying business got a little boring, so I figured we'd spice it up."

"By frightening a seventy-year-old woman?"

Her lips scrunched like she was holding in a smile. "When she threatened no more treats if we did it again, we moved on to harder targets. The guards are more fun, anyway."

Carter covered Marshall's mouth with his tiny hands. "Ssh."

Lena leaned in so her mouth was close to his ear. Her breath tickled, sending warmth down his skin as she spoke. "When we get back home, you need to overhaul your detail. They were far too easy to scare."

Why did her calling Kentucky home leave him feeling like it should be? He turned his head to see if she was joking. Everything seemed to sharpen and blur at the same time. The meadow faded away as he zeroed in on Lena. Her soft lips were slightly parted in a smile. Wisps of black hair had pulled free from her pony and fluttered gracefully in the breeze. Her no-nonsense scent of soap and the outdoors grounded him, making him feel like just a regular person again.

When was the last time he'd felt normal, like he didn't have the weight of the world on his shoulders? High school? Definitely not. His parents had pushed him so hard he hadn't had room to breathe. The Air Force? Maybe. The military seemed to be the great equalizer of people. The Air Force didn't care who your parents were or how much money was in the bank. If you had honor and worked hard, you excelled.

He was so exhausted from years of always having to be on. From fighting to strengthen the nation in DC to shifting the manufacturing business Amara had left to fully support the military, he hadn't had time to breathe, let alone pause to consider if he really should do what he was doing. Maybe it was time to give up his pursuits in the Capitol, let someone else take the torch.

"Daddy, the fox is playing."

Marshall tore his gaze from Lena and took a deep breath to focus. The fox frolicked in the field, disappearing in the tufts of grass to pop up again. Marshall envied the carefree existence the animal had. Not that he wanted to sell everything and live off the land or anything. But being able to let loose and have fun would only make his relationship with Carter stronger.

"She's playing and having fun, but she's also working." Lena pointed toward the animal. "See how she tips her head before she jumps into the grass?"

"Uh-huh." Carter wiggled like he wanted to be jumping rather than just sitting still.

"She's listening for critters she can eat, voles or other

rodents that live in the grass." Lena sighed and wrapped her fingers around the straps of her pack. "We can learn a lot from the fox. They're one of the few animals that find fun in survival."

The fox disappeared again, only this time she came up with a mouthful of rodent. Carter cheered and clapped like the thing had just won the playoffs. It darted off into the woods, but Lena's words lingered. Could Marshall find a way to have fun and yet still do all that was required of him? There was only one way to find out.

He put Carter down and grabbed his hand. "Want to pretend to be foxes? We can jump and play through the grass while we hunt."

"Yeah!" Carter squeezed Marshall's legs in a tight hug. "I love you, Daddy."

"I love you, too, buddy." Marshall patted Carter's back, swallowing down the lump in his throat.

"Come on." Carter took off, tumbling through the grass with a laugh.

Marshall followed, bending down next to Carter, who was twisting his head from side to side like the fox did. He took off again with a yip. A laugh burst from Marshall as he raced after his son, barking more like a dog than a fox, though he wasn't even sure what a fox sounded like.

He glanced back at Lena. She trailed behind them, a smile upon her beautiful face. Her gaze met his and filled him with reassurance. She took a deep breath, nodded, then scanned the area, probably for trouble.

A shriek of laughter pulled him back to where Carter had disappeared behind a lump of grass. Carter's head poked up from the greenery to the left of the tuft, so Marshall bunched his muscles and sprang over the grass. The ground sank when he landed and sent him sprawling into a boggy, moss-filled mess. Frigid water seeped through his clothes and made him shiver. Lena and Carter laughed behind him, so he flopped onto his backside and sat up.

"That's the problem with Alaskan muskeg." Lena's face radiated joy as she helped Carter to his feet, and Marshall wasn't upset that he was wet and chilled. "It can be firm ground one minute and unstable under your feet the next."

"That seems to be an Alaskan trait." Marshall grinned up at her. "Throwing me off-balance."

Would she catch his meaning? Did he want her to?

"I'd like to think of it as keeping you on your toes." Lena stepped close and extended her hand.

She helped him stand more than he wanted to admit. What looked like solid ground with bushes growing from it shifted underneath him and made it difficult to get out of. When he finally stood, his clothing stuck to his skin and sent another shiver through him.

Lena scanned him from head to toe, her forehead creasing in concern. "Let's get back and get you out of your clothes."

Her eyes winged to his and were wide on her face as a deep pink blush tinted her cheeks. He tipped his head back and laughed. Heat spread through him at the thought of her warming him up.

"You know what I mean." She snatched Carter's hand and headed back toward the cabin.

"I don't know, Lena." Marshall's voice was smug to his own ears. "You might have to explain that to me."

She turned to glare at him, but the smile that tipped her lips negated the expression. She focused back on the way to the cabin, tripping slightly on a clump of grass. He chuckled and rubbed a hand across his chest. Could it be that he left Lena as unbalanced as she did him?

Lena shook out Marshall's pants as she prepared to toss them in the wash. She'd have to contact Bjørn on the ham radio and make sure he brings up more water. If Marshall and Carter kept it up, they'd be out of water by the next day.

Her cheeks heated again with the thought of her words to Marshall. She hadn't meant it in the way it had sounded. The entire way back to the cabin, her thoughts had raced between his laughter and how amazing he was with Carter. When she thought back over the last two months, she realized she'd been unfair to Marshall. Sure, he wasn't around enough, but when he was, Carter had his undivided attention, even if it happened to be thirty minutes here and there. Earlier, Marshall had taken it to a new level with his fox impression.

Marshall and Carter's voices filtered through the wall that divided the bathroom from the utility room, their laughter settling in her bones. She twisted the jeans in her hands. The desire for laughter and family in her life warred with the need for justice. What if Bjørn was right and her bitterness pushed all hope of having a family of her own away?

Something crinkled through the fabric as she clenched his jeans in her hands. She pulled out a folded piece of paper. Setting the pants on the washer, she carefully opened the moist paper. It was fragile, more so from the obvious wear of many openings than getting wet.

She licked her lips and read the words written in neat, flowing letters. A rock settled in her stomach at what could only be Marshall's wife's begging words to forgive her. Words of terror and worry. Words that claimed she had to push him to vote for a bill she knew to be wrong to keep Carter safe. Guilt layered thick in the ink and etched understanding and pain in Lena's heart. Marshall's wife had only done what every mother would have when their child was threatened, what Lena would probably do in the same situation.

"It's my fault she died." Marshall's voice startled her, and she quickly set the note down so she didn't tear it.

"You didn't know." The letter made that clear.

"No." His voice strained as he stared at the paper. "But I knew something was wrong. I assumed it had to do with the business. I should've taken the time to ask, but I was so focused on my job at the Capitol that I selfishly figured she'd tell me if she wanted help."

"That doesn't mean her death is your fault." Lena's throat closed at the guilt he must carry, and she had added even more to him with her accusations and thinly veiled contempt.

"They targeted Amara to sway me." His humorless laugh made it hard for Lena to breathe. "Their strategy worked. She not only died because of me, but your fiancé and other soldiers also died because of my choice." He sighed, closed his eyes, and leaned against the doorframe. "I've hurt so many with that one vote, I don't think I'll ever make up for it."

A sharp pain of regret stabbed her chest, and she placed her hand against the washer to hold herself up. No wonder he worked tirelessly to support the military through his business. No wonder he still tried to change the corruption of politics, even though he no longer held a position there. He shouldn't carry all that guilt, not when so many others had been deceived too. Didn't she know just how far and deep the tentacles of the nefarious group grasped? Kiki's own parents and Colonel Johnson, a man Lena had respected, were wrapped tight in the calculating hold of those bent on twisting the government to their own desires.

"Marshall, you've already helped more than you'll ever know." Her throat hurt like she'd swallowed shards of glass. "Your work with June and her inventions and the lobbying you've done in the Capitol has tipped the scales for the good."

"It's not enough, and yet the more I push, the farther I get from Carter. I can't make up for what I did if I want to have time for him."

"When will it be enough then? When will you pay enough to make up for that vote?" She didn't know if she was asking Marshall or herself.

"I ... I don't know." He pushed his hands through his hair, hopelessness filling the small laundry room and squeezing everything good out until all that remained was its stifling weight.

"I do," she whispered.

She didn't want him trapped in the endless cycle of guilt anymore. He was a victim just like Ethan and all the others were. By lumping him in with the organization that deceived so many, she'd failed to acknowledge all he'd done the last two years. June wouldn't be able to manufacture so many of her gadgets for the military if Marshall hadn't shifted all his company's focus to supplying her the materials she needed. People in the Capitol and across the nation wouldn't be talking about term reform if he hadn't taken up the torch and pushed for it. She'd been wrong to ignore all of that.

"I forgive you, Marshall." Relief coursed through her and left her trembling. "You've shown your honor in everything you've done the last two years. I see it now. I'm sorry I didn't before."

His search of her face left her exposed, but she no longer cared. Her mother had been right. Lena needed a shift in her focus from her grief and hate to what brought hope and honor.

"I want to believe you." His rough whisper broke the last of her resistance.

"Then do." She straightened from the washer and crossed her arms over her chest.

He swallowed, glanced at his wife's letter, then returned his gaze to Lena. "Okay. Maybe I will."

"Daddy, you's said you get me a 'nack." Carter pushed his way between Lena and Marshall.

Marshall stumbled into her with a grunt, one hand reaching behind to steady them on the washer and the other wrapping around her waist. His hand burned against her side, confusing her with the intensity of its heat. Marshall's fingers flexed on her waist as he mouthed, "Sorry," and let her go. She covered her unease with a shrug and a tightlipped smile.

She might be ready to forgive Marshall for his vote. She wasn't sure if she was ready for anything more than friendship. Yet the lingering warmth from his touch, causing her pulse to pick up, called her a liar.

SIXTEEN

"OH, WHERE ARE WE GOING NOW?" Lena grabbed the book Carter handed her, and Marshall watched with rapt attention as she helped Carter onto her lap.

"On a bear hunt." Carter placed both hands on her shoulders. "Don't worry. We're not scared."

Marshall chuckled from the kitchen where he put the last of the dishes away. This entire day had been amazing, and the coziness of the cabin capped the night off perfectly. He paused to hear what Lena would say.

"We're not?" Her eyes widened theatrically like she wasn't sure.

"Nope." Carter turned around and settled in her lap. "Me will protect you."

Lena smiled and smoothed Carter's still-damp hair down. She gave him a hug as she read about catching a big bear and swishy grass. The scene warmed Marshall's heart and made it all liquid like lava. He clicked the last plate in the cupboard. At some point after Amara's death, he'd let his heart go as hard as rock. Seeing Lena with Carter, and spending time without the pressures of guilt and responsibility hitting him from every angle, had heated his core to a molten mess.

He didn't want to stay on the outside of his life with Carter anymore. He wanted to snuggle on the couch, reading books and making memories. If Lena happened to cozy up to them, too, Marshall couldn't imagine anything better. Her forgiveness earlier might just be the step in the right direction to make that newfound dream a reality.

He crossed the room just as the adventurer in the book traveled through the deep, dark wood. Instead of settling into the recliner, he sat on the loveseat with the two of them. Like a family. He stretched his arm across the back of the couch, and Lena turned a hesitant smile to him as she and Carter recited words they'd obviously read several times. How was it that a week before, her eyes had shot daggers at him? Marshall never wanted to leave this place, didn't want to leave Lena and Carter there.

Yet, he had to.

He'd been gone from his business with no communication for much longer than he was comfortable with, especially knowing some insidious organization wanted to take him down. Would he get back to reality and find everything he'd worked for gone?

He trusted Ed could take care of things, but Ed wasn't Marshall. As much as he could rely on and respect his best friend, sometimes their ideas of what the company needed varied greatly. Plus, the vote was only three days away. Marshall couldn't just leave that to chance, not when he'd dedicated the last year and a half to putting all the pieces in place for the bill to have a good chance of passing.

Could he just leave Lena and Carter up here alone? Lena could handle anything the Alaskan wilderness threw at her, but Marshall wasn't sure he could be away from

Carter for however long it would take to guarantee his safety. He also didn't want to lose any ground he'd gained with Lena.

"It's a bear!" Carter yelled, his smile stretching across his face in excitement as he peeked up at Lena.

As they rushed back through the scenes of the book, Carter's giggling voice rose in anticipation. When the story's family claimed they wouldn't go bear hunting again, his tiny forehead scrunched in thought. Just what would his son come up with this time? Marshall held his breath, waiting for what would spill from Carter's lips.

"We'd go on a bear hunt again, wouldn't we?" He lay down so his head was on the armrest and his feet stretched across to Marshall's lap. "We no be scaredy cats, would we Eena?"

"Nope." Lena smoothed Carter's hair off of his forehead, her fingers trailing down his cheek. "When you're afraid, you have to push through and do what needs to be done." This time when she ran her fingers through his hair, his eyes drooped closed. "Sometimes the fear will go away, but often it doesn't and you just have to continue through it."

"Are you ever 'fraid, Eena?" Carter's voiced slurred with sleep.

She swallowed and peeked at Marshall. "Yeah, Carter, I get afraid sometimes."

"Okay, buddy, it's bedtime." Marshall rubbed Carter's belly. "Give Lena a hug goodnight, and I'll put you to bed."

"Will you pray for me like Eena does?"

Carter's question had Marshall's eyes darting to Lena's. She prayed for his son? What didn't she do? She'd make an amazing mom someday.

"Yeah, I'll pray for you." He cleared his throat, pushing down the emotion clogging it.

Carter sat up and threw his arms around Lena's neck. "Me love you, Eena."

"I love you too." She closed her eyes and leaned into the hug.

Marshall wanted to witness that exchange every night. His desire to make them all a family reared up strong and scared him. He pulled Carter into his arms and carried him to their room.

How could he have such powerful feelings for her when he'd spent the last two years feeling nothing? Could she ever feel the same? What if he lost her like he lost Amara? The more questions that tumbled through his head, the more the fear clawed up his gut and swarmed over the hopeful feelings that had bloomed there.

What was it that Lena had said?

Sometimes pushing through fear was the only way to get to the goal.

He settled Carter into his bed, said a prayer for protection, and kissed him on the head all while his mind raced with thoughts of Lena. Marshall didn't want to go back to the hardened person he'd become. Though the feelings swirling within him made him uncomfortable with confusion and worry, they also infused him with a dream he'd thought he could never aspire to again. He desired a family for Carter, wanted siblings he could play with. Brothers or sisters with raven hair and eyes so dark he could get lost in them. After being with the Rebels, a small family didn't seem as satisfying as it once had.

Marshall stole one last look at Carter before he pulled the blackout curtains closed and headed into the living room. He paused as he stepped into the open space. Lena stared into the wood stove and pulled lazily at the end of her ponytail.

Doubts twisted in his gut, so he took a deep breath to settle them before he stalked across the space. He sat on the recliner, unsure of the coziness of the loveseat now that Carter wasn't there. He'd just gotten her forgiveness, something he never thought he'd have. He didn't want to push her trust of him by moving too fast. For all he knew, she could throw venomous glares at him or punch him in the face. If she didn't, he'd take that as a sign to move forward with Operation Charm Lena.

"We need to talk." Marshall's words caused her lips to tweak into a grin before she controlled it.

She crossed her arms, leaning back against the opposite side of the couch, and raised her eyebrow in a silent question. Or maybe it was more of a command. In either case, it made Marshall's heart pound in anticipation. He was used to being the one in charge, but he didn't think he'd have that position with Lena. She was too much of a driving force to be the yielding partner.

Would that make a relationship between them burn hot with passion or explode in conflict? He inwardly shook his head. He was getting ahead of himself. Marshall took another breath.

"Okay. Shoot." She was just going to let him talk?

Marshall stared at her, determined to catch any signs of how she really felt in her expression.

"I'm going to have Bjørn take me to an airport when he comes up to join us tomorrow." He quickly continued when her forehead crinkled in objection. "I know Bjørn had some things he had to take care of before he could come up here long-term, but now that Carter is safe here with you, I need to make sure everything is all right back home. I can't be out of communication indefinitely. I can't leave my business to others, no matter how much I trust them. Plus, the vote for the term-limit bill is in three days." He picked at nonexistent lint on his jeans. "I've dedicated too much time and sacrificed too much to just give it up when we are so close to having the numbers to pass it."

"All right." Lena swallowed and stared out the window, still bright with the midnight sun of late July. "You won't be able to come back." She turned her gaze to him. "Not until it's safe to bring Carter home. It'd be too risky. No one knows we're up here at the moment. It's the only reason Bjørn could come back. When he does, he'll be fully stocked with enough for us to last a good month or more. But you'd be going back into the bear's den. If you tried to come visit, you could be followed, and then Carter wouldn't be safe."

He had ridiculously thought he could figure out a way to visit on the sly, but she was right. He looked past her at the rocky mountaintops. Could he be away from her and Carter for an unknown time? Would he even know when it was safe to come get them? He closed his eyes as heaviness settled on him again. Responsibility and his own wants warred within.

"It's okay, Marshall." Lena scooted to the other side of the couch and stretched her hand to squeeze his that gripped the recliner's armrest. "I understand you need to finish what you've started, but I think you should call Zeke and hire more of the Stryker team for protection until the threat is contained."

He nodded, grabbed her hand, and squeezed it in a move that probably showed his desperation. "I'm scared." His voice was hoarse and scratchy as fear climbed up his throat. "What if something happens? What if I never see you two ... Carter again?"

"I'll keep him safe. I promise." Her whisper held a confidence that eased his muscles and settled his fear to a slight buzz as opposed to the disconcerting clanging it had risen to.

He ran his thumb along the back of her hand. He could trust in her strength and knowledge to keep his family safe. With them hidden away, he could focus on the tasks needed to be done to bring them back to him.

SEVENTEEN

LENA STUFFED another protein bar into her backpack and slid the water bottle in the side holder. Her plan was simple: distract Carter with a bear hunt so he wouldn't be upset about Marshall leaving. All night, she'd tried to tell herself that she wasn't disconcerted with him leaving, that she was worried about what Carter would do. She couldn't lie to herself when she broke out into a cold sweat as fear crashed over her that morning with one look at Marshall. The organization could decide to just take him out of the equation completely. She didn't want that for Carter, didn't want him left without both parents who loved him so much.

She understood and respected Marshall's need to get back. Didn't mean she couldn't secretly wish the helicopter would break, and Marshall would have to stick around a little longer. It wouldn't, of course. Bjørn was meticulous about his stuff, and his dream since high school was that helicopter. There was no way he'd let anything slip past him when it came to his "baby girl."

"Penny for your thoughts." Marshall came up beside her and grabbed a protein bar.

"I was just hoping that the helicopter would have mechanical problems so you could stay." She turned from the stuff she still needed to pack and leaned her back against the counter. "I don't want you to go." His eyes widened, and she quickly added, "It's not safe."

She turned her gaze out the kitchen window at the fireweed stalks, half-full of blossoms. She bit the inside of her cheek as worry pounded at her brain. Would the petals make it all the way to the top and summer close into a quick fall before he got back? Lena wasn't sure she could stay up in such a harsh spot if Carter had to spend the winter up away from his dad, but she didn't have a plan B.

"Hey, everything will be okay." Marshall placed his hand on her shoulder.

She stuffed the worry down and brought up her shield of strength that had gotten her through troubles. Life didn't have any guarantees of security. Letting the fear of an unknown future hinder the present wasn't the Rebel way. She could focus on the what-ifs, or she could do all she could in the now to wield the what-ifs under control.

"The minute you get to Anchorage, call Stryker." Lena used her commander voice. "Don't contact anyone else until you are in their protection."

His lip tweaked on the side as he slid his hands into his pockets and rocked on his heels. "Roger that. Any other commands?"

"Yeah." She raised an eyebrow in her best you-better-listen expression. "Figure out a plan fast. I don't think Carter will want to be away from you very long."

"Carter, huh?" His smile came out full force, dimple included, making her heart skip a beat.

"Daddy, Eena, I see the 'elicopter!" Carter dashed into

the room from the back of the cabin before Lena could respond, the stomp of his boots loud against the wood floor.

Marshall's smile turned sad as his gaze lingered on her a moment before following Carter out the door. Lena stared after them, a sense of foreboding skating up her spine. She shook it off, stuffed the remaining items into her pack, and stomped out the door. She had to show Carter that being in the Alaskan wilderness was an adventure, one he could tell his daddy all about when he returned to them.

Marshall held Carter, who stood on the porch railing. The kid bounced up and down on the narrow board in his excitement as Bjørn touched down. One thing was for sure, the boy would keep her busy. Hopefully busy enough not to worry about Marshall.

"Born!" Carter waved wildly as Bjørn climbed out of the cockpit.

"Let's go see if he needs help." Marshall lifted Carter from the railing.

Movement past the helicopter grabbed Lena's attention. She placed a hand on Marshall's back before he could put Carter down. If it was a bear, she wanted them all safely inside. She cupped her hands over her eyes to shade them from the sun and scanned the trees and brush. She swallowed as a hard rock settled in her gut. Why was she so hyped up? Animals were a part of being in Alaska.

She shrugged, hoping the motion would relax her overactive mind. As she lowered her hands, men emerged from the forest like ground wasps bursting from their hive. The rapid *pop-pop* of their guns as they fired at the helicopter sent her pushing the Rands off of the backside of the porch toward the woods. She glanced over her shoulder in time to see Bjørn bailing into the trees by the helicopter.

Would they catch him? Would they just kill him on the spot? How had they found them in the first place?

"Go into the woods," she harshly whispered as she scanned behind them, her Sig ready in her hand.

Men swarmed the helicopter, then continued toward the cabin just as she pushed Marshall into the thick undergrowth. Had they been seen, or had the intruders been more focused on Bjørn? She searched the woods where her brother had disappeared but saw nothing. She needed to move, get the Rands to safety.

The helicopter exploded in a hot billow of fire, causing her to duck and Carter to scream. Bjørn would freak. Lena took one last look as the door to her cabin was kicked in. A few men scanned the area while the others stormed into the cabin.

Good.

Lena would take advantage of the fact they hadn't been seen.

"Let's go. Stay low until we get deeper in the woods." She urged Marshall forward, keeping her hand on his back as he dashed into the dark forest.

Would she be able to keep them alive, fighting the dangers of the wilderness and an organization that seemed to stop at nothing to get what they wanted? She adjusted her pack on her back, glad that she had packed extra food for her and Carter's bear hunt. She'd just get them somewhere safe and call in the cavalry. Gunnar could extract them and find Bjørn.

Wait. The SAT phone still sat nestled in the charger. Lena inwardly groaned and stumbled over a root, quickly righting herself. Bjørn had arrived before she'd grabbed it. There wouldn't be a rescue, at least not anytime soon.

Marshall hiked Carter up in his arms as he pushed

through some black spruce that had grown thick together. Thank goodness the Alaskan terrain would hide their escape. It wasn't fun to trek through, but hopefully those after them wouldn't be able to track them as easily as they could somewhere else.

A jumble of rocks were piled before them, and Lena pulled on Marshall's shirt. "There. Stop there."

Marshall tried to put Carter down, but the child clung to his father as he sobbed. Lena felt like doing the same, which was stupid. Crying wouldn't solve any of their problems. Marshall adjusted Carter and sat on a boulder, his chest heaving.

"Did ... we ... lose them?" Marshall spoke between gulps of air.

"I think so." Lena scanned behind them, searching for movement as she caught her breath.

"Born?" Carter's watery gaze darted between her and Marshall.

"Didn't you see him race into the woods?" Lena faked a fun attitude she didn't feel.

Carter shook his head, wiping his nose across his sleeve.

"Well, he tricked those bad guys and got away." Lena wiped the tears from Carter's cheeks. "Bjørn is too smart for them."

Carter nodded and leaned against Marshall's chest. Oh, to believe so easily. Lena lifted her eyes to meet Marshall's. Why was this organization so insistent on getting him? How was she supposed to keep them safe when the organization had somehow followed them to the cabin no one knew of?

"You okay?" Her voice faltered with her doubts.

"Yeah." Marshall placed his hand on her shoulder like he could see her uncertainties piling up. "You'll get us through this."

She nodded and turned her face back the way they'd come. She couldn't let him see any more of her insecurity. He had enough to worry about and needed to trust her.

Needed to believe she could get Carter out of this and away from harm.

If it was just the Alaskan wilderness they had to contend with, she could get them to safety without hesitation. Sure, it might be hard, but she had spent as much of her time growing up exploring the Alaskan outdoors as she had staying safe at home. Throwing in homicidal maniacs who'd blow up a helicopter without pause took the adventure to a level of danger she wasn't sure she could handle alone.

She sucked in a shuddering breath. Why hadn't she allowed Zeke to send in reinforcements? Would her stubbornness get them all killed?

EIGHTEEN

MARSHALL CONCEALED his shiver as best he could and scooted closer to the small fire Lena had built. How had his life come to this, cowering in a dank cave, hiding from people he hadn't even known existed two weeks earlier? How had he missed this level of corruption right under his nose? Some kind of analyst he turned out to be.

He rubbed his hand through his hair as worry about how they'd get out of this mess alive settled with a quiver in his stomach. Escaping by helicopter was no longer an option. Had they caught Bjørn? Lena had insisted Bjørn would be okay, but Marshall wasn't so sure. Was someone else Lena loved dead because of Marshall? Why hadn't he given Carter to Lena and gone to help Bjørn?

Marshall was a coward, that was why.

As he'd trembled over his son, hoping the men hadn't seen them, the fact that he was weak had settled on him like a soaked blanket, freezing him to his core and weighing him down. Otherwise, he would've skirted through the woods to help a friend instead of barreling away as fast as possible. He would have joined with the fighting ranks of the Air

Force instead of taking the easy route behind a desk, analyzing data.

He wasn't a hero. No. People had called him that when he'd gotten out of the military and ran for office. Like a fool, he'd let them. Had let the false words bolster him until he imagined himself invincible. Now, the words burned hot in his eyes. He blinked away the tears.

He was far from heroic. Men and women like the Rebels were. Lena, who would leave her brother behind not knowing if he would be caught or not, had more courage and honor than Marshall ever would. She would never want to be with someone as inadequate as him.

He snorted at himself. He didn't deserve her anyway. She needed someone who could match her strength, someone like her dead fiancé with his special ops training. Too bad Marshall had screwed that up as well.

Rustling at the mouth of the cave tightened his shoulders and made his heart race so fast he was sure it'd explode. Was this how rabbits felt before they were eaten? *Come on, Marsh. Stop being a wuss.* He gripped the handgun Lena had insisted he keep, careful not to put his finger on the trigger. Could he even be man enough to shoot the gun?

Carter shifted behind Marshall, whimpering in his sleep. Marshall pushed his heavy shoulders back and moved so he blocked his son. Protecting Carter meant everything to Marshall. He'd do everything he could to keep him safe.

Lena stepped through the opening, and all of Marshall's muscles relaxed in a whoosh. Two birds hung from her belt. How in the world had she gotten them? She'd left the only gun they had with him. She held a handkerchief bulging with something in one hand and a long, thick spear like some mighty Amazon warrior in the other. She amazed him and reinforced every conclusion he'd come to. She'd gone out and somehow provided food for them while he'd shivered by the fire.

"I saw nothing out there." Lena leaned the spear against the cave wall and scrutinized him over the fire. "You okay?"

No, not really.

He swallowed, nodded curtly, and pointed his chin to the birds. "Dinner?"

"Yeah." Lena smiled radiantly as she handed the handkerchief to him and unknotted the birds. "God's looking out for us. These two were easy pickings, and the forest is littered with those right now."

Marshall unwrapped the cloth to reveal huge mushrooms. Here, he thought they'd starve, but she planned a gourmet meal. Just another way he couldn't compare.

"How in the world did you hunt without a gun?" Marshall set the mushrooms aside and pulled out his pocketknife, determined to help make dinner however he could.

"The perfect-sized rock and a good aim is all it takes to stun little birds." She shrugged, while his mouth hung open.

"You killed them with a rock?" Marshall sounded like an idiot, but who could actually do stuff like that?

"Well, no. I knocked them out with the rock." Lena set them on the ground and dusted her hands together. "Wringing their necks killed them."

Right, because she was some kind of superwoman.

"Want me to pluck them?" How hard could pulling feathers be?

He wished his upbringing had included more of the outdoors. Maybe if his family had spent more time hunting and camping and stuff, he'd have a better understanding of what to do. Neither of his parents had felt any desire to rough it. A week at the mountain lodge in the Appalachians with guided fly-fishing and trail rides with tame horses was the extent of their experience in the great outdoors. If they made it out of this alive, he'd have Lena put him through a wilderness bootcamp.

"I have an easier way to get them ready." Lena motioned for him to get up and handed him one bird. "We are going to stand on their wings and pull up with their feet. It'll leave us with just the breast meat connected to the wings."

Marshall squished his lips together and puffed out his cheeks. Hunting with nothing but a "perfect-sized rock," whatever that meant, and ripping birds in two was so far from his comfort-zone he wasn't sure if he could do it. He swallowed down the nausea and copied Lena as she showed him what to do. The snapping and popping of bones disconnecting preceded a kind of sucking noise as the bottom half of the bird separated from the wings trapped beneath his shoes.

"Perfect." Lena looked at him like he'd just won first prize in a spelling bee or something. "Hand me that half, and I'll go toss them in the other cave farther back."

"You sure that won't draw some wild animal in?" Marshall picked up the wing and examined the perfectly clean meat nestled between the feathers.

"I promise." Lena chuckled, like this was just another walk in the park. "Nothing's coming in or out of the cave unless it comes from that opening."

Marshall's gaze darted to the cave entrance. He hated the fear that clawed up his throat, hated the way his overwhelmed brain went numb. He wiped a shaky arm across his forehead. This wasn't him. He always had a handle on any situation, knew how to look at a problem and find a solution.

He took a deep breath and blew out his frustration. This

circumstance was just like any other difficulty he'd encountered before. Yes, the stakes of failure were higher than any other, but that didn't mean he couldn't work through it.

Couldn't push the terror down and help Lena instead of just being deadweight.

She stepped into the light, knelt by Carter, and adjusted the emergency blanket she'd packed in her bag. The tenderness of the moment filled Marshall's heart and ricocheted the longing for family against the cave walls. He'd do everything he could to work as a team and get them home. He pushed aside the doubt that questioned if it would be enough, if he would be enough.

NINETEEN

"WHAT ABOUT THIS ONE?" Marshall asked from twenty feet away where he crouched over an amanita mushroom.

"Well, its nickname is Death Cap," Lena said dryly as she adjusted a sleeping Carter in the sling she'd rigged from her things.

"Nope." Marshall straightened, kicked the red-topped mushroom, and huffed. "How is it you found enough for supper and breakfast, and I can't find a single one?"

"I just stumbled on a good patch is all."

He grunted like he didn't quite believe her. As Marshall attempted to help, his frustration had mounted throughout the morning. Sure, he didn't know north from south when it came to the outdoors, he had been in the Chair Force after all, but his trying shifted her thoughts of him even more. He'd called it his crash course in all things Lena. She smiled at the way he had said it, like it was the most important training he'd ever had.

What impressed her even more how he really focused on what she would tell him. He didn't let his ego impede her teaching him. Instead, he constantly checked what he was doing against her example, asking if he was right. Not only did he trust her completely to get them to safety, but his respect of her showed in everything he did.

She never could have imagined how attractive that was.

He moved toward her. His one-sided smile that revealed a dimple had her stomach rioting like a flock of snow buntings had just taken off. Her mom was right, again. Letting forgiveness into Lena's heart had been like a go-ahead for her brain to notice all the good in Marshall, opening a future she'd never imagined possible.

Of course, she'd have to keep them alive first.

She just had to head them toward the network of cabins set up in the Wrangell-St. Elias National Park. If a rescue didn't happen before they reached the first cabin, they'd at least have shelter as they made their way out of the park.

"Guess if dinner's up to me, we'll be eating spruce bark." He laughed, but she heard the dejection in his tone.

She hated that his shoulders slumped a little more with each failed mushroom identification. Hated how he thought he wouldn't succeed. She'd been raised in the woods, and even she didn't remember everything. Why was it so important to him to get it right? Was it him not having a clue, or was it something more? She stopped, her forehead crinkling at the puzzle he presented.

"What?" Marshall wiped his cheek. "Did I smear my face with dirt again?"

Her voice suddenly clogged at the back of her mouth, so she shook her head. She adjusted the shoulder strap holding Carter with one hand and reached out and ran the back of her fingers across his skin with the other. He stilled like a spooked caribou. How could she keep him encouraged?

Well, she could start by telling him what was growing in her heart.

She stepped closer and pressed a soft kiss to his lips. One of his hands bunched the back of her shirt like he was desperate for her touch and worried she'd step away, while the other gently cupped her cheek like she was delicate silk. Tension snapped between them as she pressed her forehead to his, their breath dancing with each ragged intake and exhale.

"Lena?" Marshall smoothed his hand across her back, his voice rough and low.

What she felt for him differed from her relationship with Ethan. With Ethan, excitement and the thrill of their secret love had laced the relationship with a constant high. That was just who Ethan was, burning hot for life, and she'd loved that about him.

Marshall left her warm all over, like he'd built a fire deep within her and he planned on camping out. He was comfort and safety, which was a ridiculous thought. She was the one who was supposed to protect him, yet with him she felt sheltered. Fortified. He'd seen the worst from her, had experienced her disdain. Still, his calm confidence and willingness to let her take the lead sang to her spirit and let her soar.

"I ... we're going to be okay." Her lips brushed against his as her whisper sent the buntings in her stomach to flip like they'd found fresh grass. "Together, we can get through this."

He pulled back just enough to search her face. She held her breath, waiting for his rejection. She'd been so cold and rude to him, he might not even want her. His expression turned from shock to determined, curling her toes in her hiking boots. He cupped both hands around the back of her neck. His kiss held urgency and hope, jumbling her thoughts up even more. His scorching touch morphed the buntings into flames.

Carter whimpered and shifted, though the whimpering may have been her own. She had to get them to safety. She wasn't quite ready to put a name on what she felt for Marshall, but she wanted to protect it, to sink her claws in and hang on like a wolverine.

"You are an amazing woman, Lena Rebel." Marshall wrapped his arms around her and Carter, and tucked her under his chin. "How ... how can you possibly stand being near me, let alone forgive me? I don't deserve it, not after the mess I made of things, the trouble I'm still causing."

She pushed back enough to look up at him. "This isn't your fault, Marshall. Stop blaming yourself." She put her head on his shoulder, glad she finally realized the fact. "My father always said that when you're doing good, honorable things, the devil zeroes in like there's a target on your back. With everything you're doing, both before that bill two years ago and after, your target must be a billboard."

His swallow was loud in Lena's ear, and he tightened his embrace. "That's the problem, though, isn't it? If it was just me, I wouldn't care how big the target was, but it's not. Shouldn't I be thinking about Carter's safety? They'll kill him just like they did Amara if they have to."

"My father also says that doing right means sacrifice." Raising her head, she stared into his eyes. "We both know that more than most. Yet, the fight for good is worth it. I promise, I'll do whatever I can to keep Carter safe. When we get back, I'll clean out your entire security detail and hire friends I have from the military, trustworthy men and women who won't sell out. Home will be more secure than Fort Knox."

She bit her lip, not sure how he'd take the next thing that was on her heart. "But, Marshall, you don't want to become the person who would compromise his morals for safety, whether your own or someone else's. You've shown how much that would tear at you these past two years."

His jaw clenched, and he looked out into the woods. Had she overstepped? Though she loved Carter with all her heart, she wasn't his mother. Would she say the same thing if her own son was in danger? Maybe growing up Alaskan gave people the realization just how difficult life was. The only guarantees this existence had were that challenges would come, but there was always hope, hard work, the love of God, and loving others.

He turned back to her, his gaze piercing deep into her soul. "Is home Kentucky, then?"

"Maybe." She swallowed down her sudden nervousness.

He slid his hand down her arm and threaded his fingers through hers. "I'd like it if it was."

"Come on." She pulled him to continue walking. She had a lot of thinking to do. The sound of calling Kentucky home, of seeing what could grow between her and Marshall, gave her a hope for the future she hadn't felt in a long time. The offer from General Paxton to join his team to take down the organization pushed to the front of her thoughts, taunting her with guilt. The idea of leaving the Rands and working for Paxton felt like ash in her mouth. "We need to keep going."

"How far is it to the settlement you're taking us to?" Marshall stepped up beside her and squeezed her hand.

"It's a ways." She adjusted Carter on her shoulder. "We'll probably get there tomorrow."

"Want me to take him?" Marshall reached for Carter.

"Nah. Let him sleep."

Most of the time, he wanted to walk on his own, but when he slept, he became deadweight. Yet she liked the feel of him, heavy in her arms.

She and Marshall walked side-by-side, their hands intertwined in comfortable silence. The wind teased the treetops above them, sending the fresh smell of pine to her. She took a deep breath, relishing how the need for idle chatter didn't exist. The forest bustled with the flapping of wings and the chattering of squirrels. Though she hated their circumstance, she had missed being in the wilderness.

The trees opened up to overlook a valley with what she hoped was Little Jack Creek below. Bright pink fireweed covered the valley floor, while charred trees stood like ghosts of their past selves, still reaching for the sky. The beauty that could bloom from destruction was evident in nature's rebirth. Would this be what her life became?

"Wow. This is gorgeous." Marshall's awe reflected her own.

Carter rubbed his nose against her neck and then glanced around, his eyes squinting in confusion. Then, as if realizing where he was, he perked up, his head whipping around as he took everything in. Lena squeezed him in a hug. She couldn't believe how much of her heart he'd taken over.

"Eena!" Carter's legs pumped against her body like he was revving up to take off. "It's a bear!"

"Hey, good eyes, buddy." Lena pulled Carter out of the sling and shifted him to her other hip to get a better look.

Sure enough, farther down the hilltop, a sow huffed, her ears turned in their direction. Lena stepped to the slope's edge and searched the hillside for a way down. They might have to go the opposite direction from the bear before they could make it to the valley floor.

"Three bears, Eena!" Carter shrieked in her ear.

Lena whipped her head to the bear. Two cubs stood on their hind legs to investigate the strange animals on their turf. A mama bear was nothing to mess with. Getting distance between them and the animals just became priority.

As she turned to motion the way she wanted them to go, the ground beneath her feet shifted. Her stomach flew into her throat in a strangled gasp.

"Marshall," she choked out just before the ground disappeared from under her feet.

The scream from Carter chilled her bones. She tucked her body around his, praying that he wouldn't get hurt. Her back smashed into solid ground and searing pain shot up her arm. The air whooshed from her lungs as darkness engulfed her.

TWENTY

MARSHALL PICKED his way down the hill, the slow pace grating at his nerves. His heart still hadn't gone back into his chest and it threatened to choke him. Carter cried as he pushed against Lena's unmoving body. His frantic calling of her name made Marshall's heart pound faster and faster with each second. Was she dead? Was Carter hurt? How would he get them to help if she was seriously injured? What would he do if they were both hurt?

"Daddy, help!" Carter's cry focused Marshall on what needed done.

"I'm coming, buddy." He jumped down from a tuft of grass, surprised when his feet hit sand. "I'm almost there."

Taking a quick scan of the hilltop, he found it empty and blew out a breath of relief. At least he didn't have to contend with bears attacking on top of everything else. The sow and cubs had shot into the woods when chaos had shattered their quiet afternoon.

Marshall slid down the sand like it was snow, keeping his balance so he didn't end up in a heap like Lena. The closer he got, the more his stomach knotted. Even from halfway down the hill, he could see the blood smeared across her face. *Please, God, don't let her be dead too.*

Why had Marshall opened his heart again? The world was just determined to rip it out. He'd brought this on her. Unless he changed his course for the future, he'd likely keep bringing pain on her. Carter, as well. If they survived, maybe he should just let Lena take Carter far away where neither of them could be harmed from his decisions.

Could he do that? Could he be unselfish long enough for them to escape? He scanned Carter as he reached the bottom of the hill and ran toward them. His son had dirt and sand covering him from head to toe. Blood smeared down his left cheek.

Tears stung Marshall's eyes. Yeah, he'd let them go. He might not survive long without his heart, but he couldn't allow them to be put in danger any longer.

"Daddy, Lena won't 'ake up." Carter ran to Marshall, tears streaming tracks down his dirty face.

Marshall rejoiced at his own son not being injured. How had he made it down the steep slope without seriously hurting something? Marshall refocused on Lena. How had she had enough time to react to protect Carter in their fall?

Marshall scooped Carter up and held him tight against his chest. "You okay, buddy?"

"Yeah. Me okay." Carter's voice hitched on a sob. "But Eena hurt."

Carter pushed away from Marshall's embrace and turned in his arms. If Carter's constant concern for others continued through adulthood, his son would do so much good. If Marshall could keep him alive long enough to grow up.

He blinked away the moisture from his eyes and dashed the rest of the way to Lena's side. Her arm bent awkwardly under her body, and blood oozed from a gash above her eyebrow. Her back arched over the backpack strapped to her, making her twist in an eerie form of yoga.

Marshall swallowed the bile that filled his mouth and kneeled next to her. How could he touch her without making her injuries worse? Setting Carter next to him, Marshall pressed his fingers to Lena's throat. Nothing. Black spots swam in front of him. *No, no, no!* He adjusted his fingers and pressed harder. She couldn't be dead. Her strong pulse bumped against his fingers, and all the tension whooshed out of him.

Laying his forehead on her chest, he took a deep breath to calm himself. The steady rise and fall of her breathing calmed him even more. He took another deep breath, sat up, and wiped his eyes across his sleeve.

"Is Eena okay?" Carter pulled on Marshall's arm.

"I don't know, buddy." He gave him a quick hug. "I think she's just taking a little nap."

Carter nodded and glanced from Lena to Marshall. "Okay."

"In fact, why don't you lie down right here and rest while I clean Lena up?" Marshall took off his flannel shirt and stretched it out on the ground a few feet from Lena's head. "You can watch and let me know if I miss any blood."

"Okay, Daddy." Carter scrambled over Marshall's lap and curled on his side. Maybe he'd fall asleep, and Marshall wouldn't have to keep the brave face on.

Who was he kidding? Carter had just taken a nap. There was no way the kid would fall back to sleep.

Panic had Marshall's eyebrows permanently attached to his hairline.

He needed to wake Lena up so she could tell him what to do. He had never been one to let others boss him around, but Lena was different. She ordered him about in a way that strengthened him. Everything about her made him better: a better dad, a more focused businessman, better at connecting with others. She even made him more critical of his analysis of situations.

Tearing the bottom of his T-shirt free, he wet it and dabbed at the cut on her head. "Lena, honey, wake up." He cringed as blood ran from the cut a little faster. "Lena, please, we need you to wake up."

"Daddy?" Carter's voice still held hiccupped sobs.

"It's okay, buddy."

Marshall rewet the fabric and turned it to a cleaner section. As he continued to wipe the grime from her face, his desperation rose. What would happen if she never opened her eyes? Couldn't people look perfectly fine but have such a severe head injury that they never recovered from it?

His hands shook as he pressed the swatch of T-shirt to her cut. Carefully, he probed her skull with his fingertips, looking for any other bumps or gashes that could explain her unresponsiveness. When his fingers didn't press into brains or soft spots, he let out a fortifying huff and glanced at Carter. His hands were folded under his face, and his eyes were wide with fear. His breath hitched like it did when he cried, and his body was coming down from the emotion.

"Lena." Marshall turned back to her and tapped her cheek with his palm. "Lena, wake up." Frustration built in his chest, binding his lungs and threatening to suffocate him. "Lena Rebel, stop playing around and get your sorry side up." He used the best impersonation of his drill sergeant during boot camp.

Lena moaned, her eyelashes fluttering on her cheeks.

She wouldn't respond to soft touches, but yelling at her got her moving? He had so much fear and worry building up in him, he could give her a verbal thrashing if it woke her up.

"Rebel, what do you think this is, nap time? Are you a preschooler or something?" Marshall leaned over her, cupping his palms on the sides of her face. "You need to stop being lazy and wake up."

"Daddy, stop being mean." Carter got to his knees.

"I'm trying to wake her, Carter. It's okay."

She moaned again, and Marshall almost shouted with joy. He took a quick look around to make sure nothing was creeping up on them while he was preoccupied. The emptiness of the Alaskan wilderness both eased his fears and increased them. He never would've thought that possible a week before.

"Rebel, open your eyes." He leaned right in her face. "Carter needs you. I need you. Open. Your. Eyes." Each word grew louder as fear tried to wrap its fingers in his scalp and pull him down beside her.

She gasped, her arm flinging out and face going wide with fear. "Carter?" Even half-dead, her first thought was for someone else.

"He's fine." Marshall caught her flailing hand with one of his own and pointed to where Carter sat. "You kept him safe."

Her entire body relaxed as her gaze found Carter, then tensed again with a scream she cut short to a whimper. A chill washed over Marshall at her pain and his lack of knowledge on how to help. His fingers shook as he gave her hand a squeeze. Carter cried and crawled over.

"Carter, stay on my shirt." Marshall quickly set his son on the make-shift blanket and turned to Lena. "What's wrong?" That was a stupid question. "What hurts?" Like that was any better.

"I don't know." Lena's voice, while calm, had panic laced within her tone. "My arm, I think."

"Okay." Marshall adjusted his position and tried to get a better look at how her arm was trapped. "What if I undo the straps from your pack and try to take it off?"

Lena swallowed, her expression full of relief at the suggestion. If he could just keep on throwing out good ideas, maybe he could help her after all. He quickly unwound the straps from the bottom of the pack.

"Okay. If I lift you up with one hand and pull the pack away with the other, will that work?" He didn't care that he needed her direction for everything at the moment. He didn't want to hurt her more.

"Yeah." Lena's shaky voice made his knees weak with worry. "Just try to keep my arm from under me when you set me down."

Right. Marshall huffed, then threaded his arm under Lena. She trembled beneath him, her breath coming in quick rasps against his skin as she bunched the back of his shirt in her fingers. He clenched the bag in the other hand and, with extreme gentleness, lifted her enough to pull the pack from under her.

Adjusting his grip on her, he moved her arm from beneath her and set her down. She whimpered against his neck before releasing her grip on his shirt and relaxing into the ground. Marshall brushed hair from her chalky skin with shaky fingers, sick to his stomach that she was in so much pain.

"What now?" He hated to ask, but worried if he didn't prod her, he'd lose her again.

Lena closed her eyes, and her forehead scrunched. Her

uninjured shoulder wiggled, then stopped. Then her leg muscle moved against his, where he touched, and her opposite foot rotated. Was she systematically evaluating her injuries? How could anyone push through so much obvious pain like she did? She opened her eyes, and Marshall leaned closer.

"I think ..." She squeezed her eyes shut again and cleared her throat. "I think it's just my arm. Everything else hurts, but nothing like my arm."

"Okay." Marshall examined how her limb hung by her side. "Is it broken?"

Lena turned her head with a wince. Moving her other hand across her body, she pressed her fingers into her shoulder. Her sharp intake of breath made his own shoulder hurt. He shook out his muscles as she continued to probe her arm.

"I think the shoulder is just out of socket." She relaxed into the ground and took a deep breath. "You're going to have to put it back in."

His stomach flipped in on itself, but he nodded. It wasn't like he hadn't seen injured people before. He just wasn't great around them.

"Grab my forearm." She motioned with her opposite hand. "We need the arm at a forty-five degree angle. You're going to pull my arm away from me, slow and steady, okay?"

"Okay." That made no sense. Why would he pull the arm away from where it needed to go?

"You'll probably need to brace your foot on my side." Lena swallowed as her opposite hand clenched and released.

He wanted to slide his palm into hers and let her know it'd be okay. She'd probably punch him in the face and tell him to stop being a pansy. She'd be right. He couldn't stomach how much this would hurt her. He took a fortifying breath, wrapped both hands around her forearm, and carefully lifted it to the angle she'd said.

"Ready?" Was he asking himself or her?

"No." A weak smile pushed her lips up.

"Me, neither."

She closed her eyes, just to have them pop open again. "Don't jerk. That could cause more damage."

Right. Why couldn't he be the one hurt, rather than the army medic who'd been assigned to special force troops? He adjusted his hands on her arm and pulled. When she slid toward him, he pushed his foot against her side. Her arm wouldn't pull any farther, and he worried he was causing more harm than good.

"It's not working." Her voice held so much pain tears stung his nose.

"Eena, you's okay?" Carter's voice held concern from where he bounced nervously on his knees like he wanted to help.

"I'm fine." She smiled weakly at him. "Just hurt. Maybe in a little bit you can kiss it and make it better."

He nodded, determination firm on his little face. "Me do tat. Me make it better."

Marshall blinked and wiped his sleeve across his eyes before rubbing the sweat from his forehead. Maybe she hadn't noticed him tearing up. Setting her arm gently on the ground, he stood, stretched his arms over his head, and scanned the area for critters wanting to eat them. He wished his son didn't have to watch this.

"All right." Lena spoke with her eyes closed. "We have another option we can try."

Marshall shook out his shoulders and bounced like he did before a game of one-on-one with Ed. What would happen if this didn't work? Would she be able to move or would they be stuck here? Obviously, she could walk, unless she'd hurt something else, but would she be in too much pain to move? Marshall rolled his eyes. She'd push through any pain and probably still do more than he did to get them to safety.

"I need you to rotate my forearm so that my palm is facing the sky and my arm makes a ninety-degree angle, like this." She moved her uninjured arm so it looked like an L. "Then, you're going to rotate it up, keeping it along the ground, until my forearm rests on my head."

She showed him what she wanted him to do, her face scrunching in pain and her voice strained. If it hurt to move the side that wasn't hanging limp, how would she be able to take the pain when he worked the other side? He did one last jump and shake, and squatted next to her, gently moving her palm up.

"Marshall."

He yanked his hands away like she'd shocked him with an electric jolt.

"Smooth motions here." Her jaw clenched, then relaxed. "This is going to produce a lot of torque, so if you jerk or force, you'll break the bone."

His eyes widened as they darted from her shoulder back to her face. She nodded and gave him a look that reminded him of his weight trainer when Marshall was exhausted and didn't want to finish the set. Rubbing his sweaty hands on his pants, he positioned himself so he could move her arm better.

"Smooth, Marsh. You can be smooth," he encouraged himself under his breath.

Lena's laugh was short and choppy.

"What? You don't think I'm smooth?" Maybe if Marshall talked, they could both relax.

He rotated her palm to point up, and she cringed.

"You have your moments." She bit her lip, and her chin trembled. "They're few and far between, but you have them."

"Hey now, that's only because I'm out of my element here." He forced indignation into his voice as he moved her arm higher. "If you wouldn't have shot daggers at me back home and actually gotten to know me, you'd see just how smooth I can be."

A crack snapped from her shoulder. Lena's agonized scream seemed to rip from her and slice through him like a knife. Her eyes rolled into her lids, and the sudden silence of her passing out filled him with more sickening dread. *Oh God, no, please.* Marshall slumped to the ground. Had he really just broken her arm and made this horrid trek through the wilds worse?

TWENTY-ONE

CARTER CRIED out Lena's name, but his sweet voice was muffled. Her eyelids weighed a ton, and no matter how hard she tried, she couldn't get them open. Carter's crying turned to screaming. She had to move, to help him.

Come on, eyes. Open.

She blinked her eyes, and brightness blinded her. Quickly slamming them shut, she groaned against the pain.

"Lena?" Marshall's voice held such concern as his fingers skimmed her cheek.

She leaned her face toward the touch. She didn't want him to worry about her. Cracking one eye open, her vision blurred on Carter sitting among a patch of fireweed. Tears streamed down his face as he held his little clenched hands in front of his mouth.

"I'm okay." Her throat hurt like she had swallowed a handful of gravel.

"Eena?" Carter scrambled to her, only to be caught by Marshall.

"Hey, buddy. We can't touch her. Not until we know we fixed her arm." Marshall's words tumbled the events that caused her to be spread out in the dirt back to her brain.

"The bears?" She rolled her head back and tried to relax, but her body hurt from head to toe.

"Gone." Marshall scanned the area.

Good. He was keeping his wits. Someone had to since the pain spiking through her kept her from thinking straight.

"Carter?" She gazed at the boy that had taken over her heart.

"He's fine, Lena." Marshall set Carter down beside him and scooted closer to her. "Did we get your arm back in the socket or make it worse?"

He ran a jerky hand through his hair, making it stick up. His pained gaze flitted to her shoulder and down her body. How had she ever thought that he was a horrible person? Any time spent with him showed just how much he cared about others. These last two months, she could've been helping him more instead of letting her anger blind her.

"Okay." She huffed out a breath and moved her unin-jured hand to probe her shoulder. "It feels like its back in. Help me sit up."

She tipped her head, motioning for Marshall to come to her other side. He stepped over her and gently wrapped his arms around her. Her muscles bunched with pain, and she did little to help him lift her. Once sitting, she leaned her forehead on his shoulder and breathed deeply to dam up the tears the movement had created.

Marshall softly ran a hand down her back and kissed the top of her head. She didn't want to move, his presence bringing a comfort she hadn't felt in a long time. Lingering wasn't an option, though, not in this open basin with little cover and the national park cabin still a good four-hour hike away.

She sighed and lifted her head. "Let's see how you did, Dr. Rand."

He snorted a laugh as he moved back to her side. "I'm definitely not a doctor."

Holding her elbow in her hand, she shrugged the injured shoulder. Pain spiked through it like a grizzly had just chomped down, but she could move it. She nodded and rotated it some more.

"It's in." She hated the tremble in her voice. Hated the weakness it showed.

"Thank God." Marshall breathed out, and his head and shoulders slumped forward in relief.

"Eena, you's okay?" Carter inched forward.

"Yeah, buddy. I'm okay." She reached to him with her good arm and ran her fingers down his damp cheeks. "Just sore is all." Cringing, she pulled her hand back to support her arm. "I'm going to need a sling."

"Right." Marshall snatched his shirt from the ground and shook it out.

Five minutes later, with her arm secure in a sling, she hiked hand in hand with Carter through the valley meadow. He chatted away like a squirrel about the bears and falling down the hill. His voice, full of excitement and wonder, pulled her in, both soothing her mind and battering her heart. Relief that he'd come out of the fall with nothing but a few small scrapes and bumps made her a little light-headed. His love and affection coupled with Marshall's trust and interest had her contemplating a future she'd thought long dead.

She put her free hand to her aching head, running her fingers along her eyebrows before shaking off her confusing thoughts. Distractions did not belong in the Alaskan wilderness. If she wanted to get Carter and Marshall to safety, there couldn't be any more mistakes. She had to push aside any thoughts of the future, and focus. Carter squeezed her arm in a hug and gazed up at her in adoration. Focusing had never been harder.

"Will we see more bears?" Carter asked as he walked hand in hand with Lena.

Marshall strode behind the pair, still a little shaken from his education in wilderness triage an hour earlier. When Lena had come around and promised him he hadn't broken her, his relief had been so immense, he almost couldn't get his tears bottled up fast enough. He'd helped her put her arm in a sling, gotten Carter a snack and water, and had repacked and strapped on the pack with this overwhelming sense of foreboding.

How would they make it out of this when their guide and protector only had one arm? Marshall couldn't kill ptarmigan with nothing but a rock. He could harvest mushrooms if she found them, but how would she have the energy to search when her very steps seemed to jar her with pain. She did a good job hiding what she must be feeling, but she couldn't mask the tension that seemed to fill her entire body. It made her movements jerky and opposite of the grace that normally flowed through everything she did.

Maybe when they made it to the cabin she hoped was downstream, it would be stocked with food and firewood and everything they'd need to survive until she was healed enough to lead them on in strength. He hoped it at least had a fishing pole or net or something that could help him be of some use. He'd become quite the proficient fly angler after spending summers at the upscale lodge his family went to every year. Of course, the likelihood of the remote cabin being stocked with anything useful was slim.

A low noise that hadn't been there before pricked his ear. He stopped and twisted his head, trying to place where it came from. Was it some kind of bird or bug flapping? He couldn't pinpoint what or where it was.

"Lena." He closed the distance between them and picked up Carter. "Do you hear that?"

He shushed Carter as Lena tipped her head to the side. Marshall tried to keep his cool since it was probably nothing, but his heart beat wildly in his chest. Her eyes widened and snapped to his.

"Helicopter." Her words released his tension in an unexpected whoosh, and his knees almost buckled.

"Then we're rescued." He scanned the wide valley dotted with trees, trying to locate the growing sound.

"Maybe." Lena's terse tone darted his gaze to hers. Her tense expression tightened all his muscles back to attention. "Maybe not."

Great. More danger and intrigue. He missed Kentucky. Missed only worrying about international business and making sure his company had what it needed to keep up with product demand. Missed the verbal warfare launched at him from the Capitol. Missed showering.

"Quick, get in those willows." Lena pointed toward a stand of brush and pulled her gun out of its holster.

He clutched Carter close and dashed to cover. His dry mouth was more suited for the desert rather than a permafrost-ridden valley floor. He pushed as far as he could into the branches and crouched with his body over Carter's. Lena kneeled before them, her gun pointed to the ground as she searched the sky.

"There." She pointed with her chin, and Marshall followed her gaze.

The helicopter crested the mountain ridge they'd just come from, moving slowly to them like some Hollywood B movie. Would they open fire and pepper the brush with bullets? Did the occupants even know the three of them were there?

"I have binoculars in the side pocket." Lena didn't take her eyes off the approach.

Of course she did. She probably had a tent and marshmallows too. The back of Marshall's neck tingled unpleasantly, and he rubbed it away. He shouldn't let her preparedness affect him. He really shouldn't ... but he couldn't help the way each new situation seemed to cut at his inability to protect them a little more. Stupid feelings, since logically, he knew that her knowledge of the woods and expertise to get them out of any situation had kept them alive, both here and in Idaho.

He yanked the binoculars out of the pack and tapped her arm with them. "Here."

She placed them to her face and stared. The longer she looked, the more his muscles bunched, ready to dash like a rabbit. Where he'd go, he wasn't sure. He scanned the open valley filled with low brush and open meadows. Maybe they'd just cower where they were.

"Marshall, come look." Lena held the binoculars out.

He set Carter down, told him to stay put, and grabbed the binoculars. "What am I looking for?"

"The person sitting in the door. I think it's Gunnar, but ... I also don't think I can trust myself." She sighed beside him. "I'm worried I'm just seeing Gunnar, because I want it to be him."

Marshall peered at the man hanging out the door. It

sure looked like Lena's brother, but what if Marshall's brain was just tricking him to think that? Another man leaned over, and Marshall's hands trembled as he lowered the glasses.

"It's Gunnar. Bjørn is with him." Marshall smiled at Lena.

"Thank God." Lena collapsed against him, her forehead pressing into his shoulder.

He pushed her hair back and kissed the top of her head. His thoughts jumbled one on top of the other. The weight of not knowing if Bjørn had made it or not lifted, so Marshall felt like he could fly, but the unknown of what they'd do next had his mind whirling like the rotors of the helicopter.

Lena lifted her head and pressed a shaky kiss to his lips. "We're going to be okay now."

Could she read his mind, or did she need the reassurance as much as he did? He cupped the back of her head, kissing her deeply. She didn't push him away. Rather, her fingers speared through his hair, and she smiled against his lips.

"Go wave them down before they fly by." As her hand slid down his neck and pushed on his shoulder, goosebumps spread along his skin.

He was glad they'd been found, glad they didn't have to worry about surviving Alaska, but he worried that what was building between him and Lena would disappear when this trek through the wilderness ended. He gave her one last peck before pushing out of the willows. He'd just have to make sure he kept them all together. Considering she didn't seem completely opposed anymore, maybe all it would take was looking at all the angles and executing a well-laid plan.

Could he woo Lena with the normal dinner dates and

flowers? He snorted as he waved his hands above his head like an idiot. Maybe taking her to the shooting range and giving her the latest gadget designed using their material would be better.

He glanced down at her as she stepped up next to him. That idea held merit. Would she be interested in helping him improve his product so her friend June could help more people? Or maybe together they could start some kind of training in self-protection and security that helped others use the safety gear to its optimum. Hoisting up Carter into his opposite arm, Marshall laced his other fingers with hers. Whatever happened, they could figure out where life would take them together.

The helicopter touched down, and Bjørn and Gunnar raced toward them. Marshall could tell the moment Gunnar noticed Lena's injury by the way his strides stretched even longer. Hopefully, he could reassure Marshall that he hadn't broken her.

"You okay?" Gunnar gently touched Lena's elbow as Bjørn reached for Carter.

"Yeah. Just popped it out of the socket." Lena wrapped her arm around Gunnar's back in an awkward hug. "Thankfully, Marshall got the stubborn thing back in."

"I just did what she told me." He extended his hand to Gunnar, who took it firmly, then pulled him into a hug.

"You three had us looking all over the place." Gunnar stepped back.

"How'd you find us?" Lena slid her hand back into Marshall's, and he didn't miss the smirk between her brothers.

"Well, got a call from my search-and-rescue buddy who said he knew someone who wanted to help." Bjørn motioned over his shoulder. "The pilot has a soft spot for lost children." Bjørn tickled Carter's belly. "Are you ready for a helicopter ride, little man?"

"Yes!" Carter hugged Bjørn's neck tightly. "Me so 'appy you's here."

Bjørn cleared his throat. "Me too, buddy. Me too."

"How'd you get away?" Lena asked as they headed to the chopper.

"Once they blew up my girl, they didn't care about me anymore." Bjørn's tone barely repressed his anger. "They bugged out, and I got the HAM radio humming and called home."

"So my cabin's okay?" Lena's hand squeezed Marshall's.

"Yeah. They didn't even trash it." Bjørn shook his head as he lifted Carter into the chopper. "Climb on in, buddy."

Bjørn followed Carter in and got him buckled while Marshall helped Lena climb up. The pilot smiled and gave Marshall a thumbs up as he flipped switches. The co-pilot leaned toward the back of the vessel and lifted his headset.

"We're really glad we found you," he hollered over the accelerating engine.

"Me too," Marshall choked out before turning in his seat to gaze out the window.

He swallowed and blinked to clear the tears that pushed to the surface. His family was safe, for now. Gunnar and Bjørn peppered Lena with questions, prodding her arm and looking at her head injury, but Marshall couldn't focus on any of it. His mind was too relieved to process everything, so he closed his eyes and let the thumping of the blades lull him to sleep. The helicopter jerked and jolted Marshall awake.

"Welcome to Anchorage." The co-pilot clapped Marshall on the shoulder as he crossed the vessel to get Carter out of his buckle.

Marshall shook his head, surprised that the Rebels were already out of the chopper and a nurse, pushing a wheel-chair, was running up. Marshall couldn't wait to see Lena's reaction. He jumped out of the door, eager to not miss what was sure to be a show, and turned to grab Carter. The co-pilot held Marshall's son tightly against his body on the opposite side of the opening, a sinister smile across his face. Icy fear crashed over Marshall.

The helicopter lifted, and Marshall lunged, snagging the skid with his hand. He yelled, but before he could wrap his other hand around the cold, hard metal, the pilot lifted with a jerk. The skid ripped from Marshall's hand, taking his very soul from him in the whipping air. He fell to his knees, his ribs too tight to breathe, as the chopper rushed away with his son and disappeared into the horizon.

TWENTY-TWO

"THEY DITCHED the bird at Walker Field." Bjørn stepped into the emergency room. "My buddy watched them land and take off in a jet less than a minute later." He pushed his hand through his hair. "He's looking into the flight route and call sign for me."

Lena's chest burned like a moose sat on it, refusing to let her breathe. Marshall paced the short distance along the wall. He kept staring at his hands and flexing them. Nothing she said could erase his failure to save Carter.

"I'm just going to take a look." The doctor who refused to leave stepped in front of her with his otoscope at the ready.

"I'm fine." Lena swatted the doctor's hand away as he flashed the light in her eyes.

She pushed off of the examination table with her working arm, cringing as pain ratcheted through her entire body. It didn't compare to the searing heat in her heart.

"We need to leave. Zeke is setting up transport, so let's get to the airfield." She snatched her pack from the chair just as Gunnar strode into the room.

"You done?" His gaze darted around the room.

"Yes."

"No," the doctor said at the same time as Lena, causing her to glare his way. To his credit, he didn't flinch. "I haven't looked at her arm yet or the abrasions."

"They're fine." Lena stomped out of the room. "We're leaving now."

Marshall stepped up beside her, his hands shoved in his pockets and his shoulders slumped. Why hadn't she stayed in the chopper until everyone was out? She'd let her guard down, and now the organization had Carter. She needed to come up with a plan, and fast.

"Marshall, we'll find him." She slid her hand down his arm, but he flinched and pulled away. "I put trackers in his shoes. Rafe is pinpointing where he is now."

"What if they hurt him? What if—" Marshall's voice cracked, and he shook his head. "What if I never see him again?" He speared her with a look so full of anguish, his pain almost doubled her over. "What kind of father lets a stranger take care of his son? Why didn't I take him out of his seat myself?"

They stopped at the curb, the cold, humid breeze from the ocean chilling her skin. She stepped into Marshall's space, willing him to not blame himself. How were they to know the pilots were part of the organization after Marshall? She'd watched the co-pilot and his jovial act, like all he wanted to do was help. She had never expected him to be a kidnapper, so why would Marshall?

"Rafe will locate Carter, I promise." Lena praised God that Rafe had been able to reverse-engineer the tracking device Piper's stalker had used on her. "The trackers in Carter's shoes are the best. We'll figure out where they're going, and then we'll go get Carter back."

Marshall paced away, frustration rolling off of him. "They might kill him before that." He turned back to her, his hands spreading wide before he speared his fingers in his hair and pulled. "I can't lose him too."

She closed the distance between them and took his hand. "If they want you to cooperate, they need him alive. That will give us the time to mount an assault."

"But how will they even contact me to tell me what to do?" His confusion showed just how unnerved he was.

"If they can find us in the middle of the Alaskan wilderness, I think they'll be able to call you." Lena threaded her fingers through his and pulled him to the vehicle Bjørn drove up to the curb in. "Come on. Let's get in the air."

As they pulled away from the curb, Gunnar turned in the passenger seat. "I've been wondering about how they set all this up." His forehead creased, and he shook his head. "The pilot acted like he didn't know where to go, but he was pretty insistent on going the way we went. We talked through possibilities, and his thoughts made just as much sense as anything we came up with."

"Maybe they were just banking on us finding them." Bjørn turned onto Tudor Road as he made his way to Ted Stevens International. "They infiltrate our troops, they don't have to work so hard."

Just like they'd infiltrated the military and sabotaged the Colombia mission, killing Ethan. Just like they'd used General Paxton's friend Colonel Johnson to get to June and her Supersuit. They influenced civilians like Kiki's family and government officials like the colonel to reach their gains, sliding their slippery tentacles into every possible crevice. General Paxton didn't need a small team to stop whoever was behind this. He needed an army. With everything she knew, how could she not join him in this fight?

She peeked at Marshall, who stared at his hands clenched between his legs. How could she not do everything she could so more families weren't destroyed?

"Yeah, but it could've taken us days to find them." Gunnar huffed.

"We wouldn't give up." Bjørn shrugged. "They—"

Born to be Wild blared through the cab, causing her to jump. Gunnar twisted in the seat and pulled out his phone. Her lips twitched as she watched him, though nothing about this situation was funny. At least some things never changed. That her brother still claimed that song as his eased her tension a little. With him and Bjørn here, she didn't have to figure this out alone.

"Hello?" Gunnar answered the call, a hesitance in his voice. His eyebrows shot up, and he handed the phone back. "Marshall, it's for you."

Bjørn swerved into The Bear Paw parking lot and slammed into a spot. Marshall's hand shook as he took the phone from Gunnar. What would they demand now? Lena placed her hand on Marshall's leg and mouthed "Speaker."

He took a deep breath, tapped the speaker icon, and cleared his throat. "This is Marshall."

"Mr. Rand, you've been a troublesome man to track down." The cultured voice of a woman shouldn't have surprised Lena with how Kiki's aunt had been running the organization's complex in Colombia, but it did.

"Well, when someone pulls a gun on my family, I take that as my cue to leave." Marshall impressed Lena with his steady voice and banter. "Where's my son?"

"Now, see, here's the thing." She *tsked*. "You keep causing problems with the changes you've made to your business, Mr. Rand, and we don't like it."

Marshall shot Lena a confused look. "So this isn't about the term bill?"

The woman's laugh twisted Lena's stomach like she was a salmon on a fish wheel. The flippancy unnerved her. Like this was all a game, and they were the pawns.

"We couldn't care less about that bill." Her tone implied Marshall was an idiot. "People are people and easily manipulated. It doesn't matter how long someone's in office. We'll still get our way."

"Then why worry about me at all?" Marshall's calm tone slipped as red anger rose up his neck.

"Because your support of Reagan MacArthur or June Paxton, whatever she's calling herself these days, is creating a headache." The laughter had left her tone, replaced with cold calculation. "Enough of this. We need to have a meeting to discuss the future of your business, Mr. Rand. You will meet us in Kentucky. Don't even consider pulling any heroics. We know where you are. We know how you think. You know we aren't afraid of making our point with force." Her voice turned pleasant, like she was talking to an old friend. "I'm craving brunch at Coles, 735 Main, tomorrow morning, eleven sharp. Their grits are to die for."

The screen went black as the call cut off. The silence that filled the cab contained so much tension, Lena could've sliced through it. They had just less than twenty-four hours to figure out a plan and get Carter back.

"That's my favorite restaurant." Marshall's whisper shattered the stillness. "Carter loves their mac and cheese."

Something about what the woman had said needled Lena. Had their enemy really known all along where they were? Was that how they had snuck up to the cabin? If Bjørn hadn't arrived when he had, the men could have surrounded the cabin without Lena even noticing. It was obvious the chopper pilots had known where to look for the Rands.

But how? How could they know exactly where to find Marshall? Lena stared at him as he flipped the phone over in his hands. Her head pounded and her shoulder felt like someone was stabbing a red-hot poker in it, but she had to push through and figure out what eluded her. Then she remembered something that Piper's stalker had said.

"Marshall, give me your wallet." She reached out her hand, her pulse increasing with each second.

He reached into his pocket. The brown leather was warm and soft in her hand as she opened it. *Please, let me be right.* She began pulling out business card after business card.

"Lena, what—"

She cut off Marshall's question. "My friend's stalker tracked her with a business card he'd given her. He'd been selling his inventions to the black market." A lightness filled her chest as she spied the same metallic threading that had been on the card Piper had. "Looks like our favorite terrorist organization liked his design."

"I don't understand." Marshall snagged the card and looked at it with wide eyes. "This is Patrick Walker's card. He's the investor from Moving Forward. I ... he's excited about helping June get more units to the military."

"Looks like he's playing both sides." Bjørn scowled as he grabbed the card from Marshall's fingers and whistled low. "This is some fancy tech."

"Yeah, Rafe said it's some of the best he's seen." Lena scooted forward in her seat, a plan formulating in her head. "Listen, they don't know that we know about this. What if we can use it to our advantage?"

"What are you thinking?" Bjørn speared her with the

satisfied look he'd get as a kid when he made up a new game to play.

"Well, if we split up and send Marshall on one plane, I can meet up with Stryker, maybe call in General Paxton's team, and get Carter before Marshall's meeting is supposed to happen." Lena's voice rose as the idea solidified in her head.

"No." Marshall shook his head, his voice resolute.

"What?" Lena's mouth gaped as she turned to him. Didn't he see this was the best way to get Carter back?

"No. I'm not leaving Carter's rescue to someone else." Marshall's determined gaze built Lena's frustration up. "If something happens, I want to be there. I have to be there."

"It's the only way to have an element of surprise." Lena tried to tamp down her annoyance.

"We can figure something else out." Marshall clenched his jaw and crossed his arms.

"What if we have a decoy?" Gunnar rubbed his cheek as he stared out the windshield.

"What?" Lena and Marshall said at the same time.

"Well, they only have to think it's Marshall." Gunnar looked between her, Marshall, and Bjørn. "What if someone pretended to be Marshall, took the business card, and acted like he was going home?"

"The decoy could wear a hat and sunglasses." Bjørn shook his finger like the plan held merit.

Marshall's jaw shifted as he thought. "I could have my parents pick the decoy up at the airport. I'm close to them, and it wouldn't be out of the norm for me to go to their place in a moment of distress. They'd play along to get Carter back."

Lena slashed her hand between the seats. "Stop. It

won't work. We'd have to have the decoy here. We can't just pull someone out of our pocket."

"Actually ..." Gunnar's smile turned Lena's stomach. "Remember, Sunny's team is back here organizing their equipment for the winter now that Denali's summit season is done. We can ask her friend Gavin if he could help. He's built a lot like Marshall."

"In fact, if Sunny pretended to be you, Lena, that would sell the ploy even more." Bjørn's words had all the men turning their penetrating gazes on her.

She didn't want her little sister anywhere near this mess, but she had to admit it could work. It was bad enough that they had pulled Gunnar and Bjørn in. What if one of them got hurt? What if involving them brought this organization down on her family?

"Lena, we'll be okay." Gunnar placed his hand on her knee. "I can tell you're worried about us, that you're pushing us away again. But we Rebels are a stubborn bunch, and when they took Carter, they brought the Rebel wrath upon them."

"Not to mention what they did to my baby girl," Bjørn grumbled about his chopper, causing Gunnar to roll his eyes.

"Okay. Let's see if the manager will let us use their phone." Lena swallowed. "I don't trust calling from yours."

Her brothers pushed open their doors and headed inside, though worry the size of a glacier lodged in her core. Would she lose everything to this organization, not only Ethan but her siblings as well? Marshall wrapped his warm hand around hers. His sorrowed expression pushed her worry to the background where it could still chill her but didn't consume all her thoughts. She might lose everything, but she couldn't let Carter and Marshall suffer any more than they already had.

TWENTY-THREE

MARSHALL SHIFTED IN HIS SEAT, the interior of Zeke's private jet closing in on him with each new detail layered on their rescue plan. Zeke and the entire Stryker team had met them in Salt Lake, and they were now strategizing as they flew to Kentucky. The flights had been long and tried Marshall's patience.

"I've tracked Carter to a warehouse on the outskirts of Lexington." Rafe Malone, a man with slick red hair and, supposedly, a genius brain, clicked a button on his computer from where he sat across the cabin and pulled up a satellite image of a rundown building onto the big screen located at the front of the plane.

"I'm going to pretend that I'm not watching you hack into the government's satellites, understanding that this isn't a regular occurrence," General Paxton said, his eyebrow lifting. The team had called Paxton via video-conference the instant everyone had gotten settled after taking off at Salt Lake.

"Yes, sir. Never done this before, sir." Rafe's smile negated his words.

Paxton shook his head as Zeke stepped up to the screen, his hand rubbing his chin as he examined the building. There was something about the warehouse that needled at Marshall's brain. He leaned forward and squinted at the image. What was it about the nondescript thing that had his pulse pounding in his throat? The pink roof of the security house at the gate drew his attention.

"No." Marshall's disbelief whooshed out in a hoarse whisper.

He stood on shaky legs and moved closer to the screen.

"Marshall, what is it?" Lena grabbed his hand as he passed her seat, startling him from his trance.

"That's my warehouse." Marshall's dry throat made his voice croak.

Zeke swiveled to him, his hand dropping from his chin. "You sure?"

"The pink roof." Marshall stepped up to the screen and pointed. His knees trembled beneath him. "Amara had it installed as a joke after a windstorm tore the old one off." He licked his lips and closed his eyes. "They killed her on her way home from there. I shut it down shortly after. It's far out of town ... and too many memories."

The cabin of the plane, which had hummed with noise and talking, fell into an eerie quiet. Frigid cold seeped into Marshall's skin and froze his muscles. What kind of sick game were these people playing?

"This is good." Zeke clapped his hand on Marshall's shoulder and squeezed. "This gives us an added advantage."

Marshall clenched his jaw, nodding in response. Whatever the reasoning behind picking his own warehouse, he'd use it against their enemies. He'd shove the irony down their throats and make them choke on it.

He turned to Rafe and crossed his arms. "All the specs

on the building, security, layout, everything, are stored on the mainframe of my company. Should be easy for you to hack."

"Easy peasy." Rafe clicked on his keyboard with a satisfied smile on his lips.

"One, two, threesy." Jake, a gruff man that had said little since Marshall and the Rebels had gotten on the plane, answered with a chuckle.

"Ay caray, we've been hanging around Eva too much." Sosimo, June's husband and the only Stryker man Marshall actually knew, threw up his hands in exasperation.

The team all shook their heads and laughed softly. Marshall scanned the men willing to risk their lives for his son. He paused on the Rebel brothers, their heads leaned in together as they whispered. Then his gaze collided with Lena's and held. Her brothers' low words drew her eyes to them. The muscles in her cheek jumped, then she went back to examining the image on her tablet. The chill in Marshall's body froze solid. What else would she have to sacrifice because of him?

"The security feed is a closed circuit. I won't be able to hijack it until I can hook in." Rafe shrugged like it was no big deal. "With dawn still an hour out from when we arrive, it'll still be dark and shouldn't be a problem getting in to the building."

Lena rotated her arm in the socket and winced at the sharp pain lingering there. Quickly needing to cover her discomfort, she grabbed her tablet and shoved it into the bag the team had packed for her. She couldn't afford for anyone to notice she wasn't a hundred percent. The plane was thirty minutes out, so they were finishing up their attack plans with General Paxton.

"My team is waiting at the rendezvous point a half mile from the target with your face masks." General Paxton leaned back in his chair, his sigh coming loudly through the screen. "I don't want any of you identified on the off chance they haven't clued into Stryker's involvement."

Lena snorted, then shook her head when Marshall turned to her and raised his eyebrow. This organization seemed to know everything about everyone. They probably knew what color of underwear each of them wore. Unless Rafe had somehow wiped clean her association to Stryker, there was no way the terrorists hadn't connected the Rand-Stryker dots.

"I buried Lena pretty deep, created a fake security business for her, so hopefully you're right." Rafe pulled at his hair as Lena nodded. Made sense Rafe would create a cover for her cover. "But these guys keep popping back up on us like a bad case of acne."

Equal parts chuckling and groaning filled the cabin. The horrible joke seemed to cue the end of the meeting as everyone began packing things up. Lena's anxiety had tightened her muscles to the point of snapping with each minute that passed. Was Carter all right? Had whoever taken him hurt him? She slowly let out a deep breath as anger and worry threatened to overwhelm her. She had to keep sharp, stay focused. Otherwise, she'd be useless during this mission, or worse, she'd get someone killed.

"Lena, I still haven't forgotten our conversation when I visited the ranch this spring." General Paxton's words snapped her head to the screen. "I still want you on my team."

Everyone froze, and silence filled the cabin as all eyes

turned to her. Heat rose up her neck, and sweat slicked her palms. Marshall shifted in her peripheral, and she willed herself not to look at him.

"I'm still thinking about it, sir." Her answer elicited grumbles from the men, and Marshall's forehead scrunched so much his eyebrows almost touched.

Paxton sat forward and poked his finger at the camera. "We could use someone like you. I'm heading your way in five, so I'll see y'all at the rendezvous point when it's all done."

"Yes, sir." Zeke ended the call.

Lena used the chaos of movement as everyone got busy getting ready to land to slip into the galley at the back of the jet. She needed a space to collect her thoughts. Since the chopper pilots had taken Carter, she hadn't had a second to calm her stormy mind. Questions and doubts built and tumbled like a building winter blizzard over the Alaskan range. She shouldn't drag her siblings into this. Would they get to Carter in time? Could her heart take it if they didn't? She feared the answers and worried if she couldn't get her emotions under control, she'd be a liability.

As she reached the galley, a firm hand snagged her elbow and dragged her the rest of the way in to the area. Bjørn snapped the curtain closed that separated the small kitchen from the rest of the cabin and turned his eyes, full of challenge, to her. Brothers. They never knew when to leave her be.

"What do you mean, you're thinking about it?" Bjørn crossed his arms, and she backed into the counter.

"Exactly what I said." Lena balled her hands at her sides, not sure if she wanted to punch him in the face or collapse into a lump and cry over her inability to protect Carter. Since crying never helped anything, she kept her arms rigid at her sides so she wouldn't give in to her first inclination.

He swung his arms wide, motioning toward the cabin. "What about what you have with Marshall? The family you could have with him and Carter? I saw the way you looked at Marshall when we found you. For the first time since Ethan died, a spark of life—of hope— radiated from you. You're thinking about throwing that away to join Paxton's team? You know how deep undercover that team is operating. You do that, you lose any chance of a life beyond revenge and hate."

"What about justice?" Lena poked Bjørn in the chest, her whisper harsh though she wanted to shout. "What about making the people behind Ethan's death and Carter being kidnapped pay for the pain and slaughter they've caused?"

He whacked her hand aside and stepped closer. Her eyes filled with tears that no amount of blinking could dry up. His face softened, and she clenched her teeth.

"What if the justice you're supposed to give is in supporting a man fighting to do everything in his power to counter this organization's attempts at weakening the nation's defenses?" He grabbed her hand and squeezed. "What if you're meant to help Marshall make his business even better so that more soldiers will have the protection June's inventions give them? You've always had laser focus, but I think you're zeroing in on the wrong thing."

"I can't ... I can't think about that right now." She trembled and desperately wanted to flee.

"But you can think about Paxton and his secret commandos?" He lifted an eyebrow in challenge. He, out of all the other siblings, had always been able to read her.

Her breath hitched in her lungs as she gazed at him. She

turned her head and stared at the wall. Didn't he realize that dredging this up now would only make it harder to focus? He pulled her into a hug, and she leaned her head on his chest.

"You love Marshall and Carter." He whispered the statement she couldn't refute. "You're willing to walk away from that?"

No.

She closed her eyes and swallowed hard.

"Maybe." Tears burned hot behind her lids. "Yes. I can't risk my world shattering again."

She wanted to snatch the barely audible words back and stuff them where they should've stayed. She didn't though. Not now. Maybe never.

TWENTY-FOUR

MARSHALL PACED the living room of the house Paxton's team had secured. The wood flooring of the rundown farmhouse creaked and groaned like it protested the abuse. The sound magnified the agony twisting in his spirit. The torture of not knowing how Carter was. The grief from Lena's evisceration of his heart.

He stopped in front of the grimy window and stared out into the darkness. How had he been stupid enough to open his heart again? It should relieve him that she was leaving before he gave her everything left within him. He wasn't.

What he wanted to do was drag her into a private spot in the crumbling house and beg her to stay with him and Carter.

He didn't.

Every second she spent coordinating with Paxton's team, every moment she ignored Marshall existed, layered more doubt that he could convince her to reconsider. Reaching into his pocket, he pulled out Amara's note and twisted the folded page in his hand. First Amara, then Carter, and now Lena, all pulled away from him by a group more shifting mist than something tangible. Could he ever hope to find happiness again if everything he loved got snatched away? How could he continue moving forward when all he wanted was gone?

No. He closed his eyes and balled the note in his hand. Carter wasn't lost to Marshall, not yet. When he got his son back, he'd turn all his efforts on doubling his business's output. These terrorists had already compromised his family's beliefs when they threatened Amara. He wouldn't allow evil to win again.

Bjørn stepped up next to Marshall, his hands shoved into his front pockets. His relaxed shoulders were the exact opposite of Marshall's. His muscles were bunched so tight, he doubted they'd ever loosen. Gunnar filled the space on Marshall's other side. Great. Marshall clenched his jaw to keep his mouth shut. He wasn't up for a Rebel pep talk at the moment.

"You doing okay?" Bjørn spoke without taking his eyes off the window.

Marshall snorted a laugh that held no humor.

"Right. Stupid question." Bjørn shifted and lowered his head.

"We'll get Carter back." Gunnar cracked his knuckles, his confident voice not easing any of Marshall's fears. "We've done missions like this one, hundreds of times. With our element of surprise, they won't be able to react."

"Don't take this the wrong way, but nothing with this group goes as planned." The words were bitter on Marshall's tongue.

Lena hollered something to Rafe about the Eyes Beyond gadget. Marshall turned his head to find her, but stopped himself with a scrunch of his shoulders and a twisting of his neck. He'd do better staring into the black night than torturing himself with watching her. The darkness suited his mood.

"Do you think she'll actually join Paxton's team?" Marshall hated the despair that saturated his voice.

"I don't know," Bjørn said with a shrug. "You'll have to convince her not to."

Marshall didn't think that would work. Bjørn nudged Marshall's shoulder and stomped off to join the others. If Lena wanted to leave, Marshall would honor her wishes. Would the memory of her ever cool in his veins, or would every thought scorch hot with the pain of losing her?

"I know things look bleak right now." Gunnar turned and leaned a shoulder on the window, his gaze penetrating deep into Marshall. "I promise you, we will get our boy back. I'm not stretching the truth when I say this team behind you is the best. Trust them. Don't let hope shrivel away." He shrugged and tipped the side of his mouth up in a smile. "Besides, I'm not about to let anything happen to my future nephew, not when he's already wheedled his way into my heart."

Marshall rubbed his neck, trying to let Gunnar's words wash over him. "You heard Lena. I wouldn't bank on Carter and I being at the next Rebel family reunion."

"She's scared and doesn't know how to handle it." Gunnar lifted his hands in resignation. "We Rebels might like to challenge life's norms, pushing past barriers to find adventure, but put us in an emotional crisis where our heart is at risk?" Gunnar's eyes lost focus like he stared into the past. He blinked and shook his head. "We tend to bolt like a startled moose, all clumsy and wide-eyed."

He clapped his hand on Marshall's shoulder. Marshall was tempted to shake the man off, but Gunnar squeezed harder. Lena's leaving was all by her choice. Marshall knew how stubborn she was. He couldn't change her mind, not once she'd made it up.

Sosimo hollered for Gunnar, and he strode away, leaving Marshall more confused than before. Could he risk letting the dream of Lena in? He didn't want to spend life yearning for her if he didn't.

"Time to go." Zeke's voice boomed into the room.

Marshall swallowed down the bile that rose up his throat. No time to think about the what-ifs now. Rescuing Carter was all that mattered. He had to keep his focus. He'd groused enough to get them to let him wait in the van, helping out over the com if he could. Could he actually stay in there when the time came? He wasn't sure, but he couldn't wait in this depressing house. His gaze caught on Lena's as he turned to go to the van. Did her eyes hold sadness or worry? She bobbed a curt nod at him, then stomped out the door. A chill raced down his spine, and he rolled his neck to dispel it. He'd trust the team to get Carter free like Gunnar had said, but Marshall didn't have the strength at the moment to hope beyond that.

TWENTY-FIVE

LENA FLEXED her fingers next to her side and darted her gaze down the street toward where they'd parked the van with Marshall inside. What a fruitless act since it was zero dark thirty and pitch black, and she couldn't see the vehicle. A breeze blew through the tall grass meadow where they waited to breach the warehouse. It lifted her ponytail and cooled her sweaty neck. If only it would cool her nerves as well.

Why did Marshall have to insist on coming with? Why couldn't he have stayed with Paxton's team where it was safe? Sure, they had approached the parking lot in such a way that anyone watching wouldn't have seen them, and, even though it made her stomach knot, the surveillance post was the perfect spot for him. With his military analyst background and knowledge of the warehouse layout, it would keep him involved but also out of harm's way.

Paxton's team had decked the van out with surveillance cameras, so Marshall would know if anyone approached. It wasn't like he was inept at weapons. He'd handled the Sig

Zeke had given him with ease and familiarity. They all wore June's Supersuits, even Marshall, but they still had vulnerabilities like, say, a bullet to the head. Lena closed her eyes and breathed out the image of Marshall getting shot out of her mind, only to have Ethan's dead body replace Marshall's.

Tingling started in her chest and spread through her limbs. She wanted to rush back to the van, grab Marshall, run away, and hide forever. She wanted time to speed up so they could get this over with. She wanted ... she didn't know what she wanted. She snorted softly. When had she started lying to herself? She knew exactly what she wanted, to hold and love the Rand men for the rest of her life, however long that ended up being.

"We're in." Rafe's almost inaudible words came over the com and sent a wave of nausea through her.

She swallowed the burning down, slid her Eyes Beyond on, and fell in line behind Bjørn. On silent feet, she rushed through the door and split away from her brother, heading down the opposite hall. They would continue to divide into smaller teams as they methodically searched the building's few offices and storage closets, ending up in the warehouse's large production room.

Praying they found Carter in some office somewhere with only a guard or two seemed too hopeful, but she did it anyway. Then someone could retreat to safety with Carter while the team took down the terrorists.

"Clear." Sosimo's voice came through the com.

Lena peeked around the corridor, found it empty, and motioned for Jake to go ahead. He rushed down the hall to the manager's office at the end. As she followed, she scanned with the Eyes Beyond through the walls for any heat source on the other side.

Zeke grunted, then his voice echoed Sosimo's from their point on the other side of the building. "Clear here too."

Lena's pulse drummed in her ears, drowning out all other sounds. *Please let Carter be in here. Please,* she begged as Jake reached for the office door's handle and looked at her. She adjusted her grip on her assault rifle and gave him a nod. With coordinated moves, he opened the door, and she swooshed into an empty room. Her heart sank at the last hope of getting Carter out without him being in the middle of the confrontation. She moved farther into the room to make sure she wasn't missing anything, but the space held nothing.

"Clear." She swallowed down the lump in her throat and turned to the door.

"Copy. Phase two." Zeke's low mumble steeled her nerves.

The main warehouse had three entrances from within the building. Marshall had explained that while the smaller equipment had been moved, the room still held shelving, bigger machines they hadn't needed at the other facility, and a row of cubicles by the front entrance behind a divider. A large open area that had contained the packing area was positioned near the middle of everything. While Sosimo and Gunnar cleared the cubicles, the rest of the team were to work along the far edges of the room until they cleared the shelving and machines surrounding the open space.

Lena scanned through the wall as she and Jake approached their point of entry. When nothing registered, she reached for the handle and slowly opened the door for Jake to peek inside. When he nodded, she pulled it the rest of the way open and followed him into the room.

Light permeated through the shelving from the open

space, making her squint through the special eye gear. She slipped the Eyes Beyond to the top of her helmet and took a deep breath, blowing it out slowly to ease her nerves. The murmur of voices and a high-pitched cackling sound filled the otherwise tomb-like silence. The smell of dust and disuse tickled her nose, and she wrinkled it to keep from sneezing.

Jake signaled one way, so she went the other, following the shelving to weave toward the light. How did they not have guards set up? Were they that confident Marshall would do what they said that they'd only leave a handful of people? Or was it a trap—funneling everyone to one location? She stumbled and leaned against a shelf.

Scanning high and low, she searched for anything they may have missed. The darkness shifted in the rafters and a faint shimmer flashed before it disappeared to black. Her hands shook as she yanked the Eyes Beyond back over her eyes. A heat signature shifted brightly in the dark ceiling. She darted her gaze over the rest of the rafters, finding two more people stationed on guard.

"Three assailants in the rafters," Lena whispered into the com.

Marshall cursed low, his harsh breath vibrating through the earbud. "There are two ladders to the catwalks. Northeast and southwest corners."

"On it." Jake came back, and Lena watched his shadow dart past the shelves toward the corner.

"I've got this one." Bjørn echoed Jake from the team's vantage point on the opposite side of the room.

Lena took one last scan with the Eyes Beyond into the dark corners of the building. Her hands slicked with sweat, and she angrily rubbed them on her jeans. This mission held too much importance, too much of her heart, to screw it up with nerves.

She ignored the anxiety muddling her mind and looked back up to where the men hid in the rafters. How could she approach the open area without getting in their line of sight?

She turned back the way she'd come. Could she use the large equipment Marshall said was still there to hide her? *Slow and quiet.* She repeated her instructions in her head until her heart no longer threatened to choke her.

"In place." Zeke's voice ratcheted her pulse right back up.

Lena didn't allow his words to force her to rush and make a mistake.

"Here too," Gunnar replied.

Lena rolled her eyes. Of course, she was behind, but getting to her point without being seen was more important than speed. She'd just have to tell them to hold their horses.

"I'm almo—"

Gunfire exploded the silence into chaos.

"Contact." Sosimo's tight voice pushed her to move faster.

Brightness filled the warehouse as the overhead lights sprung on. She slipped behind a large machine bolted in place. The scrape of a foot across the floor behind her caused her to dodge. Pain exploded through her injured shoulder, almost buckling her knees. She followed her body's reaction and bent low, spinning on the balls of her feet in a crouch.

Her attacker's arm skimmed the top of her helmet, knocking off the Eyes Beyond she'd pushed there. Lunging at the man, she rammed her assault rifle into his groin. She cut off his high-pitched, airy squeal by crashing the butt of her rifle to his temple.

Quickly bending to him, she yanked zip ties from her

pocket, secured his hands and feet behind him, and shoved him under the machinery. She inhaled deeply to slow her breathing and rolled her aching shoulder as she scanned behind her for any other attackers. Seeing none, she continued toward the commotion.

"Jake? Bjørn?" Zeke grunted.

"Two down," Jake answered.

Lena dashed to another piece of machinery and ran to the end of it. She peeked around the edge to the open area that had been set up with a few couches and a dining table. Zeke and Rafe fought hand-to-hand with multiple attackers. Could she take one or two out from here? She shook her head. Not without hitting her men.

Bullets pinged, and she shifted to see Gunnar and Sosimo in similar positions. Successive firing sprayed Sosimo and the man he fought. Lena tensed as Sosimo jerked and went down. Marshall darted from a shelf to Sosimo's side, and Lena's vision tunneled. No, he wasn't supposed to be here, couldn't be in the middle of all this.

"Bjørn, now!" Zeke's yell startled Lena, causing her to focus.

A man snuck up behind Marshall with his gun raised. Lena aimed and shot in one smooth motion. The man fell without Marshall even knowing.

"Last one down." Bjørn's ragged voice whooshed her breath right out of her.

Gunnar finished off his attacker and rushed to Sosimo's side. Was he already dead? Had the organization left another brokenhearted home? June was due to have her baby soon. What would she do if Sosimo was dead? Lena shook her head, scanned the area behind her, and refocused on how to proceed. As Rafe and Zeke neutralized their assailants, a man stood from the makeshift living area with his back to her.

"Enough!" His voice boomed through the warehouse, and Lena sucked in a gasp.

Where did she know that voice from? He yanked Carter from the couch and held the boy in front of him with a gun to Carter's head. Lena barely controlled the primal urge to dash out and rip the man's head from his body.

"Ed?" Marshall stood, his voice thick with disbelief. "What are you doing?"

Lena's teeth clenched the inside of her cheek to bite down the anger at the backstabber. Ed Ross had been Marshall's best friend since college. Marshall trusted Ed enough to have him run the business when they went into hiding. Lena reeled at this betrayal. What must Marshall be feeling?

"Isn't it obvious?" Ed's voice dripped with disdain.

"No. It's not. Why are you with these terrorists?" Marshall moved forward with jerky movements, his hands up in surrender.

"Let's just say their plans make sense, more so than your insipid attempts at reformation." Ed's hatred spewed with each word as Zeke and the team inched forward. "Stop where you are, or I'll shoot the kid."

"Daddy?" Carter whimpered.

"It's okay, buddy." Marshall's tone roughened as his eyes narrowed on Ed. "I'm just chatting with Uncle Ed."

Ed hadn't turned around to check his six. She leveled her gun on him. One clean shot to the head and this would be done. Her hands trembled. If she missed, she'd shoot Carter. Could she take Ed by surprise without hurting Carter? Marshall's step faltered as she came out from behind the machine. She snuck toward Ed, praying with each step that he wouldn't turn around.

"Why stay with me, then? Why not just leave?" Marshall continued moving to Ed.

"My association to you has been beneficial these last three years." Ed shrugged one shoulder. "Leaving would've been counterproductive, especially after you started supporting June and her endeavors. It paid to have someone on the inside, someone who could access her facilities." He shrugged. "Someone who could compromise the quality of your product to her."

"Three years?" Marshall's hands dropped and his expression widened at Ed's statement. "Amara ..."

Lena gritted her teeth. Marshall's best friend couldn't have been a part of Amara's murder.

"Was too easy to manipulate. You too, for that matter." Ed shook his head and gave a humorless laugh. "She almost ruined everything. Came to me in tears about being black-mailed and how she was going to tell you. I couldn't let that happen."

Pounding banged in Lena's ears. When she got her hands on this traitorous piece of dirt, she'd make him pay. She slid past furniture, Carter's quiet sniffles galvanizing her forward. How could she get Ed to point the gun away from Carter's head?

"We're clear from up here." Jake's low tone came through the headset and eased down her spine.

So there was only Ed left to deal with. Her lips twisted into a sneer. Now to just take him down. She didn't care whether that was dead or alive, though Paxton would flip if she lost him an informant like Ed.

"You killed Amara?" Marshall's nostrils flared.

Lena picked up her pace, worried he'd do something

stupid, like get himself killed. She couldn't lose someone else that she loved, not when she'd just found a chance at happiness again.

"I tried to make you see reason, but, no, you had to stay on your high horse." Ed dripped with such condescension, Lena wondered how he'd ever hid his duplicity.

Marshall's chin shifted as he clenched his jaw. "You make me sick."

"And you've never had the balls to do what needed done," Ed spat back.

Lena was so close she could smell the sharp tang of fear emanating from Ed. She just needed a distraction, something to get him to point the gun somewhere else. She gazed at Marshall over Ed's shoulder, hoping she could communicate her need, but Marshall's hard stare never left Ed's face. Marshall took another step forward, his eyes narrowing on Ed.

"So, what, you hide like a coward behind women and children?" He took another step closer and spread his arms wide in challenge. "Why don't you come at me head on, without the protection of a three-year-old?"

"Better yet, why don't I just kill you?" Ed shifted the gun to point it at Marshall.

Lena darted forward. Wrapping her left arm around Ed's neck, she snaked her right hand down his outstretched arm, grabbed his wrist, and pulled up. He growled and bucked against her, but she held tight, twisting his hand back. As he bent forward, lifting her off her feet, pounding footsteps rushed to her. Her body flipped up over Ed's back as a shot blasted loud in her ear. White-hot pain seared her head, then she fell over his body into darkness.

TWENTY-SIX

MARSHALL STARED at Lena's small hand held within his and slid his fingertips along her smooth skin. His gaze roamed up her arm and to her face, peaceful in sleep. He'd almost lost her. His gaze moved across her to where Carter slept soundly beside her. Marshall had almost lost them both. His throat threatened to close again with the memory of the gun to Carter's head and watching Lena land on her back on the hard warehouse floor, blood running from her head.

He shuddered, took a deep breath in, and set his forehead on the side of the bed by their joined hands. Gunnar swore the bullet had just left a crease along her scalp, and that the bump to her head from landing headfirst would be a bigger pain. Marshall wasn't sure now. Should he have insisted they go to the hospital instead of hiding away in the safe house Paxton had set up?

Lena had said she'd be fine, that she just needed to sleep it off. Marshall had highly doubted that as he'd winced every time Gunnar had pulled another stitch through her head. He still doubted it three hours later as he watched her rest.

When they'd arrived at the safe house with the Stryker team and Rebel boys, Sosimo, bruised from the bullets that had slammed into his chest, had gone into one room, while she'd immediately gone into another. Marshall had wanted to follow her, to pull her into his arms and beg her to stay with him. Instead, he had let her close the door with a sad smile as he had rubbed Carter's back. Ten minutes later, when Carter had wanted Lena, Marshall took that as his chance to convince her. She'd been sound asleep, so he'd let Carter crawl into bed with her and snuggle up, soft snores quickly coming from him. With tears stinging Marshall's eyes at the picture the two made, he had pulled up a chair and hadn't left his post since.

He couldn't, not when his entire world was right before him.

How was he going to show her life with them as a family was worth the risk? He couldn't lose her. Had nearly died himself when that gun had fired. He sighed and gently kissed the top of her hand.

Tentative fingers speared through his hair, sending a thousand bolts of lightning down along his scalp. He turned his head and rested his cheek on her hand. She smiled softly at him as her hand trailed from his hair and fluttered back to the bed. Man, she was beautiful. He wanted to spend every morning waking up with her beside him.

"Marshall?" Her eyebrows pulled together in confusion. "What are you—where's Carter?"

He kissed her hand one more time, not taking his gaze off her. Her eyes warmed and her fingers flexed in his palm. The reaction lifted the corner of his mouth.

"There." Marshall pointed with his chin to the other

side of the bed where Carter sprawled as Marshall leaned toward her. "He wanted to see you, and since that was all I could think about too, I let him."

He set his elbows on the bed next to her and brought their intertwined hands to his face. Closing his eyes, he kissed her fingers to bolster his nerves. *Here goes nothing.*

"Lena." His voice came out a harsh whisper. "Please. Carter needs you."

Her eyes narrowed.

"I mean, that's not what I wanted to say." He huffed and shook his head. "I'm screwing this up. Yes, Carter needs you, but I need you too."

"Marshall." She shifted, trying to push herself up to sitting.

The tone of her voice settled like boulders in his gut. She wasn't going to stay. The realization sucked all oxygen from the room as life without her stretched out before him. He cupped her cheek with his hand, stopping her movement.

"Lena, I can't lose you. I'll do anything you want. If my business puts us at too much risk, I'll sell it." He leaned closer. "You want to move to the wilds of Alaska to live off the land? I'm all in. As long as I can do life with you, I don't care where we are. I love you, Lena Rebel."

Lena placed her fingers on his lips and sat up. Marshall swallowed. His heart jackhammering in his chest made it difficult to breathe. She slid her fingers over his bristly beard that had grown in over the last week, sending heat to his fingers and toes.

"Shh, Marshall. I'm not going anywhere." She leaned her forehead on his. "How could I when everything I never knew I wanted is right here with you and with Carter?"

His entire body sagged in relief, then it tensed as fireworks burst in his heart, throwing those spiraling off-shoots through the rest of him. She wasn't leaving. Hope and love burned so brightly within him, if it was actually light, it'd be blinding.

He tilted his head and captured her lips with his. It wasn't the tender kiss he'd meant to give, but one of relief and passion. He wrapped his arms around her waist and pulled her closer. He needed more Lena. Would never in a thousand years be able to get enough.

He'd been on life support before her. Just going through his days on automatic, missing out on what he'd been given in his son. With her well-placed barbs and pointed glares, she sparked him back to life.

She pulled him to sit next to her on the bed and tunneled her fingers deep into his hair. He was a goner, packed into a rocket and shot into space, gone. He kissed a trail along her cheekbone, then explored below her ear and down her neck. He didn't need the Alaskan wilderness to be stranded. He was lost in the wonder of Lena Rebel.

"Daddy?" Carter's sleepy voice shut Marshall's passion down faster than NASA's control with a no-go.

He pulled back and stared at Lena, his chest heaving as he reined himself in. Lena's eyes twinkled and her mouth twitched at the side. Marshall wanted to dive right back in. As if sensing what he was thinking, her head tipped back and a joyful laugh he hadn't heard rang from her. She kissed him again, then turned to Carter.

"Come here, squirt." She pulled him from the covers and wrapped him in a big hug.

Carter squealed with happiness and wiggled as Lena tickled his side. She flashed a smile up at Marshall that settled the chaotic sparks of earlier to hot embers. He didn't care how or why he'd been blessed with forgiveness and a second chance. He'd take it, let it make him a better man, and find a happiness he never thought possible again. His cheeks hurt with his smile as he leaned forward, gave Lena a lingering kiss, and then nuzzled Carter's neck with his whiskers until his son giggled and shrieked.

EPILOGUE

LENA CLOSED her eyes and breathed in the crisp Colorado mountain air, so different from Kentucky's humidity. The last month since they'd gotten Carter back had been a whirl of bringing on an entirely new security detail, going over Marshall's company with a fine-toothed comb, and assessing what their next step would be. She relished the chance to relax for the weekend away from everything.

She still couldn't believe Ed had been key to so much that had gone on over the last two years. Through all of Paxton's interrogations, Ed kept his lips tightly sealed, but according to Kiki's mom, who fed Paxton information in return for a lighter sentence and protection, Ed was instrumental to the organization's actions. Through another assistant within Congress, he had gotten advanced notice of the rescue mission where Ethan had died and had given the organization the go ahead to sabotage the mission. He'd pushed not only Amara, but other people close to lawmakers. He'd even been the one to pressure Colonel Johnson to betray his nation and best friend. Ed's capture made Paxton hopeful they could finally make some leeway into taking down the organization, something Lena was more than willing to let Paxton's team handle.

"Who wants to bet our man Jake here passes out when he sees Chloe step out of that cabin?" Rafe's joke opened Lena's eyes just in time to see him go all rigid, like he was in shock, and stumble backward.

"You speaking from experience?" Jake rolled his eyes and crossed his arms, but nothing could hide his smile under his trimmed beard.

"Yeah, kind of convenient you eloped with no one to witness your own foolish reaction to Piper." Sosimo chuckled and pulled June closer to his side, rubbing her very large belly in the process.

"We'll have to ask Piper to spill the beans when we're done here." Samantha turned to Tina, who snuggled up to Milo. "Why hadn't we thought to make her before?"

Lena missed the girls nights the others would drag her to when she'd lived at the ranch. She wasn't into romcoms and gushing about men, but being included, even reluctantly, had mended a part of her heart. Just like Zeke and the team had when they pulled her into their fold.

Tina shrugged. "Maybe we were too wrapped up in the romance of a beach wedding."

"Mama, I thought we were throwing confetti, not beans." Eva bounced in her seat next to Zeke.

"We are, squirt." Zeke rubbed her head. "Spill the beans is an expression."

Lena had missed this, her family of friends. They'd forced themselves in when all she had wanted was to disappear within her grief. Her eyes stung with tears, so she blinked to clear them, gazing at the tall mountains that surrounded the summer meadow Chloe and Jake had crash landed in that winter. She'd get through the wedding without crying, even if she had to wrestle her tears into submission.

"Eena, me hungry." Carter looked up at her from her lap. "Me want beans."

Laughter echoed through the trees and up the jagged mountainside. Then suddenly quieted as Jake froze, his gaze on the cabin. Lena turned, and a darn tear broke loose. Chloe walked with Piper and Davis on each side of her toward them. Lena had seen the simple, short dress covered with a long lace overdress that was perfect for their spunky Chloe, but watching Chloe radiate as she practically dragged Piper and Davis down the aisle overflowed Lena with a sense of blessing and love.

Marshall squeezed her hand, rubbing his thumb over the simple engagement ring he'd given her the day after they'd gotten Carter back. He had said he wasn't waiting long and that she'd better figure out what kind of wedding she wanted fast. She peered up at him as he lifted their joined hands to his lips and softly kissed her ring.

"Soon, this will be us." His whisper in her ear flitted butterflies in her stomach that soared to her head, making her dizzy.

Lena leaned into Marshall as she pulled Carter closer to her. She couldn't wait to marry this man and officially be a family. She might just take a cue from Rafe and elope. She smiled as Jake stepped forward, took each of Chloe's hands in his, and kissed them with precious reverence. Another tear escaped, but Lena didn't care. Happiness sprung like a deep well inside her, and she wanted the world to see.

If you want more of the Rebel family, be sure to order Bjørn's story in A Rebel's Beacon.

You can also read Arne and Katie's second chance at love in A Rebel's Heart, exclusively available for free for a limited time to Sara's newsletter subscribers.

ALSO BY SARA BLACKARD

ABOUT THE AUTHOR

Sara Blackard has been a writer since she was able to hold a pencil. When she's not crafting wild adventures and sweet romances, she's homeschooling her five children, keeping their off-grid house running, or enjoying the Alaskan lifestyle she and her husband love.

Made in the USA
Coppell, TX
20 August 2021

60900896R00111